IMMORTAL WAVES

ISLAMIC TERROR THROWN BACK

IMMORTAL WAVES

ISLAMIC TERROR THROWN BACK

By Eric Laurie

ISBN 978-1-8479947-1-4

CHAPTER ONE

I am pacing the galley's Quarterdeck, thrilled to be in temporary command of such a marvelous ship. I glance out on the quayside and am astonished to see a swarthy well-built man naked except for a rag of a red shirt come stumbling onto the edge below, hotly pursued by stone throwing citizens. In blind panic the fugitive skids and falls thrashing into the water. Clearly he can't swim but manages to grasp the foot of the galley's gangway. Scrambling onto the lowermost step he heaves himself upright and runs up onto the Quarterdeck to confront me. The mob can't follow him except by taking the same plunge since the Sailing Master immediately slackens away the stern lines and a gulf opens up between ship and shore. This prevents the maddened populace from having easy access over the galley's stern.

I am shocked to see that the fugitive is Hassan, one of the slaves belonging to my father, Francesco Valente. The enraged citizens are howling for him to be put back on shore. By bellowing loudly to overcome the row I manage to learn what the trouble is. Hassan - well behaved kitchen hand for eleven years - has been left alone to get on with his work in my family's house. The other servants are all down by the shore to see the galley's departure. The weather is very hot and Hassan wanders out from the kitchens into the street. He comes across a simple young girl left unaccompanied. Long dammed up lust swamps all caution. He carries her into the seclusion of the monastery temporarily abandoned by the holy residents. But the friars are now returning and haul him away from the girl. They have alerted returning street dwellers including the girl's parents and brothers. I realize that he will be stoned to death if put ashore, so I play for time, asking pointless questions and trying to pacify the furious mob from my place on the Quarterdeck. Hassan is cowering at my feet. A scuffle behind me makes me glance over my shoulder. I see Murad, my bodyguard, an ex-slave master lent to us by the great shipyard of Venice, wielding a whip. Thrusting me aside roughly, he flourishes the whip at Hassan and the vengeful crowd below is roaring, “Flog him! Flog him!”

The citizens of Capo d’Istria are almost all assembled to see our galley christened Leona and blessed by our Bishop before sailing. The day has gone slowly, filled with so many novel events and protracted farewells.

Leona has been rushed through a four-month building program. My fellow citizens are proud indeed that they have created this splendid thing, and sad to see it leave and take so many of their men with it. They wander on board, to stand on the Quarterdeck under the white canopy fringed in gold with a great red cross on its upper surface. They strain their necks to look up at the lateen yards, each half as long as the ship itself, and at the main peak where flies the lion ensign. Some even wander forward up onto the raised rambade deck and down onto the long iron ramming beak. As evening comes they reluctantly take their leave and go ashore, some tearfully and after many repeated parting and reaffirmed goodbyes.

The galley is at last ready for sea and waiting, moored stern to the jetty at the bottom of the street: she is waiting for Domenico del Tacco, the Galley Commander and the other galley officers to return from a farewell party. Now they are arriving: I hesitate. The crowd is baying for Hassan’s blood. Before I can stop him Murad drags him across the deck and suspends him from a lashing on the mast. I have never known a man with such powerful arms and shoulders as Murad, although he is very short legged. He is flogging Hassan with relentless savagery. I throw myself at him, bearing down on his whip hand. Some rowers come to my assistance so that I am able to wrench his whip away and throw it into the harbor.

Del Tacco orders the bleeding Hassan to be cut down from the mast, and the crowd on the jetty have to be content with his shout down to them that he needs another rower anyway and will keep Hassan on board, making his life hell.

Thus so inauspiciously, begins the first part of our voyage from Capo d’Istria across the Northern Adriatic to Venice to join the Venetian Fleet.

We are clear of the harbor now and I am going forward to take up my allotted station in the bows. Now that the stress of our departure is over and the sensation caused by Hassan's animal outburst is quieted I have time to reflect on the events of the afternoon; such a cataclysm in minutes has Hassan has undergone. Yet amongst all classes, again and again, one hears of men who become victims of imperious nature and it is the most righteous who fall into the deepest disgrace, priests with neophytes, physicians with those they are called upon to heal. Some have behind them long years of kindness and service to their fellow men. Yet their severe professional disciplines make the swing to crime more impassioned and the obloquy greater once the floodgates of desire are opened. I fervently hope this will never be my fate.

CHAPTER TWO

It is night and we are well out to sea. I am leaning over the galley's prow fascinated by the way our long ramming beak slices the black water into phosphorescent hills as it probes on into the night.

The Venetian Sailing Master attracts my attention by touching me on the shoulder;

"The Galley Commander asks to speak to you in his quarters, Ser Valente."

He glanced out to the northeast. I know that he is worried that the wind we are waiting for, the Bora, has not come. From the position of the Guards of the Lesser Bear I see that it is already midnight. Venice lies fifty miles to the West. The galley is seriously undermanned. Ninety men strain at forty-foot oars on rowing benches that are designed for close on one hundred and forty. They are tiring, and longing for the first hint of a breeze to ruffle the raven sea so that the great lateens can be spread on fore and main masts. Then they will be able to rest. The wind will take the galley, and the heavily laden stone-carrying galleon that we have in tow can be slipped and left to proceed under her own sail.

Unless we reach Venice speedily, or at least get ourselves into the range of her patrolling war galleys, we shall all be butchered by marauding Muslim pirates. These approach from the south, leaving a trail of blood and fire through Adriatic coastal towns. They are daring closer and closer to the sea entrances to the Venetian Lagoon, their ships weighed down with bleeding and broken captives.

Danger threatens from the north too. The Islamic overland advance encourages pirates based in the lagoons near the ancient port of Aquileia to extend their range of operation. Their light craft swoop down putting dozens of cut-throats on board unprotected ships, and on board single galleys without soldiery like ours, or merchantmen such as the heavy ship dragging at our towline. Appearing in an instant out of the darkness, disappearing after a few moments of horror, they leave behind an untidy shipload of carnage stripped to the skin.

To go to the Galley Commander I stride along the raised centre gangway of the galley where on either side rowers ply their exhausted frames over ever-heavier oar looms. On the gunwales to port and starboard are the quiet figures of the officers, Giovanni di Giovanni and Pietro Gravisi, their eyes anxiously trying to penetrate the dark band of mist that separates starlit water from the limpid starry heavens. They dread a rent in the veil and unleashed terror. Further aft the drummer on the Quarterdeck who normally beats time for the rowers remains silent. The sound of drums travels far over still waters. And, of course, the great stern lantern remains unlit.

Domenico del Tacco, the Galley Commander, is waiting for me. He sits at a bare table in his cabin below the Quarterdeck; his young face is sharp in the light thrown up by a candle set deep in an iron bowl. As I sit opposite him he leans forward with a seriousness warranted by some weightier problem than that now on his mind:

"Marco! The Sailing Master tells me that he is worried about the girls. He says that they are wandering around the ship. They are bound to cause fighting amongst the rowers unless they are kept inside. The men cannot pay much attention to them now, engaged in rowing as they are, but when the ship settles down under a breeze.........." He hesitated, as always trying to put things courteously. "Then there is your man. I don't mean your servant - the other...I was intending to refer to the one who unexpectedly joined us this afternoon - your runaway slave."

"Hassan will behave now, Domenico," I assure him, "and you need extra hands."

I am amazed that in our present dangerous situation Domenico del Tacco can worry about such trivialities. I mentally curse Hassan for not choosing some other time to yield to his lust, and for then obtaining sanctuary on board this galley. My family's affairs are already too well displayed by the stone-carrying ship tugging at our stern. That impediment threatens to place all our throats under the Muslim sword tonight,

"I had not expected such strong representation of the Valente interests to accompany this galley to Venice, Marco."

"Well," I reply, hoping to make light of it, "let us see. There is Osvaldo, my servant........."

"Obviously I am not objecting to your having a servant although you would be better off with a more contented one. Osvaldo came pleading to me to be put ashore before we sailed. Did you know that?"

"No. I am sorry, but it is my father who insists that he sail with me."

"Well, don't let him display his femaleness around the ship. Keep him out of sight."

"Very well, I will do that, Domenico."

"Oh Yes. There's Murad too! That's another from the Valente household. I assume that he is on board as part of my ship's company, and not as another of your personal servants. You must see that he understands that."

I regret having Murad on board. He is supposed to look after me, at my father's insistence. He has given me trouble several times in recent months because of his uncouth manner towards the men that my father has contributed freely to help in the galley's construction. Murad is a captured Turk, an ex-slave master, and a gift from my Venetian Senator uncle, Marcantonio Sanmichele. Relationships are friendlier in our shipbuilding yard at Capodistria than they are in the great Arsenale at Venice. There Turkish ex-slave masters are allowed to bully Venetian workmen. I will not let this happen in our shipyard and do my best to protect the Capodistrian workmen. They are all friends to me.

The problem of Murad dismissed for the moment, I thought it well to anticipate what might be Del Tacco's next objection, so I said,

"Then there is the cargo ship loaded with stone that you were requested to take in tow..."

The intention was only to get it clear of Capo d'Istria harbor. Then the northeast wind should have taken it. It still will when it comes up.

"That cargo is a matter between your father and a Senator of Venice. I can hardly question that."

Unhappily I know that he must be questioning it. Everyone in Capo d'Istria has questioned it. Although without my father's money the ship under us would never have been built, it was tactless of him to abase Capodistrian pride by demanding that their lovely new galley should start her maiden voyage towing stone from his quarries. Domenico del Tacco, as Galley Commander, must feel this more keenly than anyone but hesitates to put his objections into words. Relationships between his family and mine, the old and the new nobility, aren't easy. My father's arrival amongst the wealthy in one generation had been too quick to digest. His Byzantine gestures have often caused alarm amongst the older families. A fresh example of this is the purchase of two Circassian girls from the slave market at Trieste. I am taking them as presents from him to his brother-in-law, my uncle, Marcantonio Sanmichele, the Venetian Senator for whom the stone is intended. No doubt Del Tacco thinks as I do - that two wanton young slave girls will not fit well into the sombre household of a Venetian statesman.

"I will see that the girls behave, Domenico."

"They brought wine on board."

"I will see that it is thrown overboard."

"If there is any left!"

Although sensing the hostility of the del Tacco family felt towards my too successful father, I am bound to defend the presence of the girls, although I admit that the explanation was a lame one.

"Since the Prefect of Capo d'Istria wouldn't give me command of this ship it was my father's idea to engage Senator Marcantonio Sanmichele's help in getting me the command of a galley of the Venetian Navy. I have a letter for him, and the girls are a token of my father's good will."

Domenico del Tacco doesn't even smile.

He knows well that all my father's wealth and property - the whole of the city of Capo d'Istria north of the Piazza, and the shipyard, the quarries, the vineyards - cannot prevail over the claim of either an eligible Gravisi or one of the Tarsia-Tacco family to command this galley. It is simply a matter of family precedence. No doubt he thinks this will hold for Venice too, but he doesn't comment.

"How was I to remain studying in my father's library, or needlessly supervising quarries and the shipyard when Venice is collecting all her forces to fight the Muslims, and so defend Europe?"

"Naturally you couldn't continue with that, but command is a different matter," replies Domenico Del Tacco coldly, "Remember this: you have so far lived a privileged life under the protection of a rich father. Your knowledge of the world outside is very limited, and all the books you have read will be of little service in most of your dealings with others. Now help by taking responsibility for these people you've brought with you. The Sailing Master has enough on his hands, and my officers are untrained as yet. We must present an orderly appearance when we arrive in Venice - if we arrive".

CHAPTER THREE

As the Galley Commander and I silently weigh each other up across the flickering candle the Sailing Master enters the cabin, addressing del Tacco without ceremony, for so the Venetians are accustomed to behave with Capodistrians. "I intend to stand down one third of the rowers. The wind doesn't seem to be coming up and a third must rest for an hour, and then relieve another third and so on. The rowing is suffering. Without the drum it becomes ragged."

While saying this he stares at me at length, full in the eyes, probably intending to convey his contempt for the stone-carrying ship, which is jeopardizing the lives of us all. As his eyes hold mine, we feel the galley shudder under our feet following a great thump on the stern, and simultaneously came the trumpeter's call summoning the officers. Domenico del Tacco jumps to his feet and, buckling on his sword, precedes us up to the Quarterdeck.

Alarm, then puzzlement, then joy: we realize that a great puff of the Bora has brought the Valente galleon's bow rudely up against the galley's stern. Her sails are already spread. Her captain's apologies are lost in the thwacking of the heavy foresail that his men are trying to bring under control. Our men, directed by Giulio Cesare Muzio, are hauling hand over hand to bring in our heavy towline, which the galleon had slipped. They drag it swiftly on board and flake it down on the Quarterdeck. The Sailing Master himself takes the helm and brings the galley's head up into the wind to allow the lateens to be hoisted, then orders the oars to be brought inboard. Soon we are back on a westerly course, the sails bellying out to port and the ship heeling over healthily. Grateful rowers, relieved from their labor, bring out bread, meat, and flasks of wine. Some just lie down where they are and go to sleep. It is to the rambade and ramming beak that I direct my thoughts. It occurs to me that by remaining on the rambade, the high foredeck, I can keep watch on all the constituents of the Valente establishment, ensuring that they give no trouble. Murad and the slave girls are now in the compartment below the rambade deck and Hassan is on one of the forward rowing benches. Osvaldo is with me. So the Valentes are all in the fore part of the galley. At the same time, staying here, I can help the ship's officers by keeping a lookout forward. When the sails of a galley are set one cannot see ahead very well on the lee side from the command position, the Quarterdeck. I tell Domenico del Tacco what I intend to do and he seems pleased.

I am going forward and am about to climb the steps onto the rambade deck when I here a groan coming from where Hassan lies on the foremost starboard rowing bench. I go closer and see that someone has thrown a blanket over him, still bloodied from the earlier thrashing. Osvaldo is following me. I send him for fresh water and cloths, and when he returns I raise Hassan to a sitting position to bathe his flayed back and remove the caked blood. I throw the remnants of his red shirt, which is still his only garment, over the side. Then I send Osvaldo back to my quarters for one of my shirts. I tell him to bring some wine.

Osvaldo comes back, foolishly bearing the wine in a silver goblet on a silver salver, presumably thinking it is for me. I am in the process of handing the goblet to the now naked Hassan when I become aware of giggling behind the curtains that screen off the compartment below the rambade, a few feet away. As I recall what Domenico del Tacco said about the Circassian girls coming on board with wine, the curtains part, and before our unbelieving eyes the flaxen-haired elder one steps out, every detail of her slender nakedness cut clear in eyes now accustomed to the starlight. Laughing, she skips up the rambade steps, turns at the top, provokingly faces us for some moments executing sinuous oriental dance steps, and then slips blithesomely over onto the ram to relieve herself of so much wine.

I am pushed aside by an enormously aroused Hassan who - it must be remembered - has been dragged unsated from his afternoon passion. Now, pain of flogging forgotten, his monstrous member erect, he up rears his rampant self and, consumed with lust, strives frantically to mount the rambade steps in pursuit of the girl. He is frustrated by nearby rowers who force him back to his bench. The same curtains part again and Murad appears from inside - his official quarters are below the rambade - with shackling irons in his hands. Within seconds he has skillfully secured Hassan by the left ankle to a ringbolt placed below the rowing bench expressly for shackling slaves.

The girl comes back down the rambade steps and, as she parts the curtains, she gives me a sidelong look and slants her eyes towards the interior invitingly, managing also to convey her distaste for the agonizingly thrusting and gloating Hassan. Brought up to cruelty, a slave girl knows well how to torture a slave.

Throughout this I am holding the goblet of wine in my hand. I now hand it to Hassan who takes it and spitefully throws the contents in my face. Osvaldo sadly wipes the wine away from my eyes and I look up to find myself facing Domenico del Tacco's disapproving stare. I explain what has happened. He merely says coldly, "Murad is not a slave master on board this ship, whatever his function may have been in the Valente household. I have no slaves. And tell him to keep out of the girls' quarters."

I send for Murad and gave the order perhaps wrongfully denying him some ancient perquisite of slave masters. If it had he would not have been able to explain this, for his tongue was cut out long ago. So for the second time that day I am obliged to humiliate him in front of the galley's crew. He accepts the order, scowling and stumbling away amongst complaining rowers.

A sense of his mad thirst for vengeance comes through to me and something holds me back from going down those few steps to take advantage of the girl's offer. I should have given more thought to Murad. Instead, I am excited by Hassan's too conspicuous lust, and I am thinking how convenient it would he if I had brought Gabriella with me - Gabriella, daughter of my widowed father and a serving woman, Milka, who so assiduously encouraged the girl to give herself to me to spite my father. Monkish abstinence is an aspect of galley life I have neglected to take into consideration and the future seems bleak of opportunity.

As I fight a lonely battle with my lower self, Osvaldo emerges from the darkness with my velvet cloak and my quadrant. The cloak, he explains, is to protect me from the night air. And the quadrant? Even Osvaldo must realize that we know our position too well to require a celestial bearing, even if this mode of navigation were in common usage among Capodistrian sailors, which it is not. In fact, the quadrant came to me through one of my father's merchant captains, who had brought it from Lisbon together with the navigation tables in

Latin. Since these tables were based on daily solar altitudes at Lisbon and were intended for voyages from Portugal south along the African coast as far as the Equator they were of no use in the Adriatic, and it was my intention to inquire whether Venetian mathematicians had produced tables based on noon observations of the sun at Venice to find latitudes useful in our locality.

Naturally Osvaldo has no interest in all this. But I think he is aware of the temptation for me that lies in the compartment below. Perhaps, because he is an effeminate young man, with a girlish figure and swaying hips that bring jeers from the rowers as he prances up and down the centre gangway, he senses my craving and has some notion of giving me an occupation to keep me out of trouble. I tell him to take the quadrant back to my cabin and to get some sleep. As he leaves I ask him to call me at dawn. I've no intention of remaining on the rambade deck much longer now that the galley is well on her way, her departure from Capodistria seemingly undetected by Muslims from the south and other pirates from the north.

Soon I feel the deck heave and slope away to port as orders come from the Quarterdeck to shorten the sheets to bring the ship closer to the wind. The Sailing Master is altering course to north-west to compensate for the galley's drift to leeward under the influence of the current in the west Adriatic. This will ensure that we make a good landfall, near the San Nicolò entrance to the Venetian Lagoon.

As the galley's head comes around the bowl of heaven turns above me, and there on the starboard are the seven great stars of the Wagon part of the Great Bear. I automatically follow the pointers, Merak and Dubhe, to find the Pole Star and think, as I have thought many times before, that Calypso's instructions to Ulysses to keep the Wagon on his left so that he would reach Greece from her island must have been based on the assumption that the Wagon revolves about its own centre; and this is not the present situation.

Before going below I stare out into the night for some considerable time. I hope to be the first to spot any enemy. In fact I have far less to fear from out there than from the twice slighted Murad lurking in the darkness of the rowing deck below, his hatred of me gnawing the more deeply since, tongueless, he was bereft of the solace of communicating his troubles to his fellows.

CHAPTER FOUR

Osvaldo fails to call me at dawn. I notice that the galley's sails are furled and the inboard oarsmen only are rowing keeping one third of the oars moving slowly to hold the ship's head up into a light breeze.

The Galley Commander, the other officers, and the Sailing Master are intent on watching an approaching boat and pay no regard to my late appearance. I am glad since only now do I realize that my doublet is far too garish for the deck of a war galley, especially in the fresh light of morning. My father's tailor, one of those who treat young men as though they were girls selected the color, I am ashamed to say, to match my eyes. Now, like a fool, I stand there on the deck of this warship in a green doublet, the sleeves slashed to reveal a yellow underlay. It is cut low at the neck to show to advantage the undershirt, gold edged at the collar, and lace cuffs. Were the tailor been I would have thrown him over the side for in the boat approaching are Venetian officers clad in simple leather jerkins.

We are safely close to Venice. Her war galleys are in sight and the Campanile of San Marco, its base still below the horizon, mocks the fear that haunted the night. The Venetian officer mounting the gangway announces that he has come from Fort San Nicolò which guards the entrance to the Venetian Lagoon. He tells Domenico del Tacco to take the stone-laden galleon in tow again. She has furled her sails and is drifting near us. In clipped tones he commands,

"The galleon is to be anchored just inside where you will see others waiting. She will be sunk there to block the entrance. Your galley is to proceed into the Laguna and anchor off the island of San Giorgio which faces the Doge's Palace across the entrance to the Grand Canal. There you are to prepare the ship for a visit from the Doge, and wait for instructions to approach the Piazzetta which will come later in the morning. The Venetian Navy will organize the ceremony for the Doge's visit."

"But the galleon is loaded with stone contracted for by the Signoria of Venice," objects Domenico.

"Then her stone cargo will be all the more useful for blocking the entrance against the enemy if the time comes," replies the Venetian.

Glancing with contempt at my doublet he asks me, "Are you Nicolò Sanmichele's cousin, Signorino?"

"I am Marco Valente," I reply, to point out that I am a person in my own right and not just some Venetian's cousin, "although I do have a relation here called Nicolò Sanmichele."

The young Venetian steps down into his boat without a backward glance, peremptorily ordering his men to cast off the line.

"That's foolish," I turn to Domenico del Tacco. "They cannot sink that ship, and that cargo. My father.........."

"They'll sink us if they want to," interrupts del Tacco impatiently. "Since your Senator Uncle, Sanmichele, controls the Venetian Navy and gives this kind of order you had better discuss the question of that stone with him. For my part........." He didn't finish: the Venetian officer is shouting over the stern of his departing boat. "The Muslim, Kara Hodja is reported to be sailing towards Venice with forty galleys,"

"The Valente family has a lot to learn." The Sailing Master addresses del Tacco, turning his shoulder on me. I remark to myself that what little respect the Sailing Master has for Capodistrians seems to have evaporated now that Venice is in sight.

We close on the galleon and inform the rueful captain of her doom, then take her in tow again. As we approach the entrance the buoyed chains are drawn back to allow us through. We leave the galleon at her last anchorage and under the Sailing Master's directions proceed into the Laguna where we anchor as instructed - off the island of San Giorgio.

I am entranced at the sight that confronts us as we float at anchor on the sparkling plain of the Laguna. So often what we have joyfully anticipated in life proves a disappointment. As a boy I visited Venice in a bragozzo, kept below deck by a younger and sturdier manservant than my present ever-whining Osvaldo and was transferred straight to the Academy I was then attending. Now from under the gold-trimmed awning of the galley I see this ancient and lovely city as though for the first time.

Even the radiant candor of early morning light scarcely gives credence to the dream-created palaces fringing the canals and interpenetrating the peerless Venetian sky, still innocent of the horror that lay over the horizon. Each mansion seems entirely self-sufficient in its own luminescence yet integrated in some vast architectural concept, a magic osmosis of the exotic Levant and the Gothic deprived of Nordic gloom, a mirage that must surely fade as we draw near. The Doge's Palace, confronting us across the water, abode of immense and ruthless power, seems to rest serenely, pink-lozenged and buoyant on its airy substructure, the lace-like quatrefoiled ogival arched loggia. Even we rebellious Capodistrians must tremble lest this city ever be sacked and put to the torch by the Muslims.

The Venetian Navy takes over the galley efficiently and drafts the entire Capodistrian crew into the Arsenale, replacing them with uniformly dressed Venetian oarsmen. They leave the Sailing Master in charge under the nominal command of Domenico. The galley is scrubbed down from stem to stern. The sail stoppings are rearranged along the yardarms according to Venetian Navy regulations. The ropes are scrubbed white and perfectly flaked down on the decks. As morning advances we are grateful for the shade of the awning while we wait for the order to move across to the Piazzetta, where we can see drummers and trumpeters are taking up their positions between two tall columns, gay with enormous flags. Framed between the gold fringe of the awning and the gilded Quarterdeck balustrade the scene is like the page of a gorgeously painted book except that the characters move. I can hardly wait for the time when the galley will float across the Laguna so that I can step ashore and into that painting.

Presently, we discern that something from that scene is moving across the Laguna towards us. A gondola arrives at our gangway and another of those leather-jerkined, steel- accoutered Venetians steps out. He mounts the gangway purposefully, salutes del Tacco perfunctorily, and makes straight for me. I don't recognize my cousin, Nicolò, at first. I suppose I was expecting the same boy that I last saw five years earlier. Nicolò said afterwards that he found it difficult to recognize me since he too was looking for a boy and not a man, but since the Sanmicheles are expecting me in that ship it could not have been too difficult to know which one was I amongst those on deck.

I am hardly an inconspicuous figure in that unfortunate doublet. Nicolò gives me a cousinly embrace and tells me that his father has sent him on board to welcome me. I ask him to convey my compliments to his father.

"You will soon have the opportunity of presenting them yourself," he replies brusquely, nodding towards the Piazzetta, "He is the person responsible for this ceremony, and he certainly requires some successful show of this kind if he is going to survive politically through the next few weeks. I have come on board to talk to you personally. Can we go somewhere more private?"

Del Tacco and the others have courteously drawn apart from us, but I think it advisable to take Nicolò below deck to my cabin, since I too have something important to say, and to say very emphatically, which is that come what may I have no intention of getting involved in Venetian politics. I have so far done little of what my father hopes for or expects of me, but I am determined to obey his absolute prohibition against any involvement in Venetian politics. It was too obvious that as one of those families not listed in the Golden Book, although very wealthy, we could only lose against the Venetian patrician class. I explain this to Nicolò, and I also tell him that I am here with a letter and the gift of two slave girls, hoping that his father will get me command of a Venetian galley.

"Why serve in the Venetian Navy, Marco? My father could get you a lectureship or some sort of post at the Academy. He has a very close association with the Rector, Loredan. Do you remember him?"

"Thank you, but I've had enough of learning."

Still, the idea is tempting. Often as a schoolboy in that Academy I admired the libertine life of some academics, swilling wine in the Piazza San Marco prior to a night's romp in the deliciously immoral and forbidden Egyptian quarter. I know my father won't agree. It has taken him long to approve my choice of the Navy, but now he is set on it he won't change his mind. If I as much as suggest it he will accuse me of playing a trick on him simply to get to Venice. Anyway, serving in a galley, I will be in Venice most of the time and free to do what I want and without the censure of the irreproachable Rector Loredan. I don't say this to Nicolò though. Instead I explain,

"Besides, learning can be dangerous these days."

"Dangerous!" he laughs. "You think the Navy's not dangerous? But perhaps this war scare won't last. The Holy League won't hold together."

He picks up my quadrant and begins toying with it as he tries to explain to me the international situation.

"The Navies will fall out as they did last year, and the Venetians will have the most to lose. The Venetian Navy will find itself unsupported in the Eastern Mediterranean since Spain is heavily occupied with unrest in the Netherlands, and English attacks on her trade routes. The Papal forces don't amount to much. We Venetians will probably try to relieve Cyprus in the face of a vastly superior Ottoman fleet, and fall into disgrace again. Only this time it will be the new Commander-in-Chief of the Navy, Sebastiano Veniero, who will suffer. The last one, Hieronimo Zane, died in prison after his failure. Did you know that?"

I take the quadrant out of his hands since as to emphasize his last remark he bangs it on the cabin table. I stare at him blankly.

"I suppose you haven't heard that the terms of the Holy League were finally agreed upon and the treaty signed in Rome fifteen days ago?" he queries.

"What are they?" I inquire, to show a polite interest, "I am afraid that I know even less about international politics than I do of Venetian ones."

Nicolò is eager to tell:

"Under the Holy League Treaty the force mounted to meet the Otoman will consist of two hundred galleys, one hundred supporting craft, fifty thousand infantry and five hundred cavalry. It will be supplied by Spain and Venice principally, although the Pope, Mantova, Savoia, Parma, Urbino, Toscana, Ferrara, Genova, and the Knights of St John occupying Malta will also contribute.

"The mission of this force is vaguely defined but it is obviously seen as a maritime operation, and the role of the cavalry is not evident. Its inclusion has already given grounds for questioning Spanish intentions. The Spaniards have insisted on a clause allowing operations against Muslim Tripoli, Tunis and Algiers.

"The composition and whereabouts of the Ottoman Fleet cannot be ascertained with any reliability, but some intelligence reports put its strength as far higher than the numbers of the Allied forces. Since Spain is to contribute the main bulk of the men she gets three shares of the spoils in event of victory, whilst Venice only gets two shares and the Pope one. For the same reason, I suppose, the command of the enterprise has been given to Archduke Don John of Austria, bastard brother of the King of Spain and hardly any older than we are ourselves. He will never hold this force together.

"Admiral Veniero, the Venetian Commander-in-Chief, is at the moment conducting operations against Muslim pirates in the southern part of the Adriatic. My father dispatched a fast light galley only yesterday with the Senate's firm instructions that Veniero is to put his forces at Don John's disposal. Veniero has requested permission to take independent action and sail to Cyprus to relieve the Venetian garrison at Farmagosta, now under heavy siege.

"I cannot imagine the ancient Veniero, with his temperament and long years of command, working happily under a boy Commander-in-Chief. Still less can I imagine him working with the Genovese Gianandrea Doria - not after the way Doria let down the Venetian Fleet last year. In the Pope's mind there is some outdated and romantic idea of a new Crusade. Venetian naval power may be sacrificed to this. This would favor the political interests of Spain, which has always tried to weaken our hold on the Eastern Mediterranean and destroy our commercial prosperity. She wants this more than does the Ottoman. Are we Venetians going to let the Pope and Spain throw away our Navy in such a silly venture, and end up economically ruined?"

Nicolò's eyes flash as he bangs the cabin table with the flat of his hand to emphasize his words. I am glad that I have taken the quadrant away from him. He clearly expects some comment from me but I have nothing to say, not having learnt about these things. But I am secretly pleased to discover that such grandiose military preparations are in progress, that war really is coming. I begin to imagine the glamour and glory of battle.

At this point Nicolò's efforts to educate me are interrupted by a messenger from Domenico del Tacco who comes to tell us that the order to approach the Piazzetta has been received and that I am required on deck.

CHAPTER FIVE

To measured drumbeats the Leona slides over the scintillating Laguna towards the quay beneath the Doge's Palace. Three ship lengths off the Riva San Marco the rowing ceases on a double drum beat, the anchor falls, and the Venetian Petty Officers in silent co-operation and with absolute precision maneuver the oars so that the galley's stern comes to rest quietly alongside a pontoon ceremonially laid out with a purple carpet and railed with gilded stanchions and tasseled cords.

The Piazzetta is crowded with people, soon to be ordered roughly aside by the ubiquitous leather-clad young Venetian officers. Alvise Mocenigo, the Doge, approaches from the Palace, dressed in a voluminous cloak of cloth of gold, and horned biretta. Several Senators, amongst whom I recognize my uncle, Marcantonio Sanmichele, tall and austere in a purple cloak, accompany him. The trumpeter sounds a call that brings the galley crew upright, eyes level, and oar looms so dipped that the oars rest uniformly at right angles to the ship's side and at an angle of fifteen degrees above the horizontal. I am late in buckling on my ceremonial sword that Osvaldo hands me as an afterthought. I catch a look of impatience from del Tacco, who tells me to follow him down the gangway onto the pontoon and up the broad steps onto the Piazzetta.

The Doge, standing under a column surmounted by a winged lion, puts forward his right hand and del Tacco inclines over it, half bending the right knee. I follow and imitated this salute and then turn to Marcantonio Sanmichele who gives me a formal kiss on the forehead and not too gently pushes me aside. The Doge and his entourage move to the edge of the jetty, looking down on the Leona. Someone, presumably the Provveditore of the Arsenale, is explaining to the Doge something, probably his construction policy. As Nicolò suggested what is being staged is something of political significance in

Venice and has little or nothing to do with our Capodistrian home. After about twenty minutes the Doge and most of his retinue depart.

Marcantonio Sanmichele is on the point of accompanying them when he remembers me. He inquires after my father, who fell badly whilst going the rounds of some quarries and, having subsequently contracted chest trouble, is still unwell. Sanmichele says that a man of my father's age and wealth should delegate such duties to others. I thank him for sending Nicolò on board and hand him my father's letter. Taking it he turns his back on me, but I still have a duty to perform and seek to awaken in him some further interest by shouting after him that my father had sent him two girls.

"Slave girls! Well, bring them out! I would have preferred the gift of one of his quarries but I suppose Michaela will know what to do with them. You must come and see your cousin, Michaela, before she takes the veil and goes from us for ever."

He turns away to give some order to an attendant. I thought his last remark very strange. Michaela is Nicolo's sister, a year or so younger, who usually stays with her mother at the Sanmichele's country villa on the Terraferma at Noventa near Padua. I remember her as a joyful little girl. Admittedly I have never known her well in the sense that I know Gabriella but cannot imagine why she has decided to go into a convent. Going down to the galley I call the slave girls and out they came, shy and open-mouthed at the surrounding splendor. Sanmichele's gondola comes to the pontoon to take charge of them and I and Nicolò return on board the Leona which is being rowed along the Riva degli Schiavoni towards the Arsenale.

The great gates in the high crenulated wall of the Arsenale open to admit the ship into the first basin. At first glance we seem to be moving through a formidable fleet of galleys but a closer look reveals that they are mostly derelict with defective upper parts that indicate that the hulls too have probably been neglected. Having traversed this basin we enter a short canal between vast lofts and arrived in another, smaller, basin in which there were a few, perhaps a dozen newly painted and well fitted ships. We have come to the place reserved for us amongst these. When we have moored with the stern to the jetty the Venetian crew begins to go ashore and our own Capodistrians to return. I tell Osvaldo to get some men and follow me with my chests, and set off with Nicolò who shows me the hospice where I am to be accommodated temporarily while still attached to the Capodistrian galley, Leona.

I notice, regretfully, as we pass them, that the Capodistrians look a rather untidy group after the smart, uniformed Venetian sailors. With them is Murad who holds Hassan by a short chain as though he is a performing bear. As we pass Murad acknowledges Nicolò with something not far short of an obeisance. This seems very strange. However, I reflected, Nicolò has been explaining on the way that he is one of the Guardia della Notte, the young officers responsible for law and order in the city. His particular duties cover the Doge's Palace and neighborhood, as arranged by his Senator father, my uncle. Murad may have had this pointed out to him and wants to ingratiate himself with someone connected with law and order. The head steward comes forward to show me to my room on the first floor, overlooking the basin, and Nicolò and I follow him there. Osvaldo arrives with the men bringing my chests and the quadrant. I send him for water so that I can refresh myself, telling him at the same time to find out where we can get some food.

Osvaldo is away a lengthy time, probably trying to find a Venetian volunteer who would come as my servant in his place. Nicolò takes advantage of his absence to try to interest me again in politics, and is well into an explanation of the policy of his party called the 'Young Nobles' who are French 'sympathizers', or so he expresses it. He is explaining that the best interests of Venice lie in a separate peace with the Muslims rather than prostitution to Spanish interests when Osvaldo returns panting, bringing the water and news that food and wine are being laid out on the refectory table, that the Signori are already gathering there. He adds that there is much hilarity over the fate of someone's galley. He commences a rambling account of what some of the servants have said. I tell him to keep quiet, decide to forego washing, and Nicolò and I set off for the dining hall to find out for ourselves what this is all about.

As we ear and drink by attentively listening and with the help of replies to a few politely phrased questions from Nicolò we are able to discover the complete story. It appears that one of the Signori, now absent from the table, a noble by the name of Augusto Contarini-Colonna, haughty and immensely rich, having been appointed Galley Commander has over some months spent part of his fortune in fitting out his galley. He bribed merchants to divert to his usage the most expensive woods, fine white cordage, paints and gold leaf, and a splendid canopy. He employed wood sculptors and other artists to embellish the ship which became the envy of less wealthy Galley Commanders who were waiting for scant supplies to trickle through to them.

Recently as summer advanced Contarini-Colonna acquired the habit of spending weekends with rich cousins in their villa amongst the hills at Montebelluna. There in a large marble-colonnaded courtyard, surrounded by exotic shrubs and Greek statuary, they would pass the clear warm evenings reviving the culture of an earlier generation, singing Petrarchesque stanzas to the accompaniment of lute and viol. On a Saturday, for instance, one of the guests would be designated as the antagonist of love, denouncing it as the source of pain and progenitor of all the ills of mankind. After some hours and recourse to delicate dishes and light wines, another would come forward as the champion of love, naming it the source of all joy. This would all take some considerable time, and the party would be resumed on the Sunday afternoon. Then, in the guise of a wise hermit, another guest would set out to show that neither definition was entirely right: compounded from carnal desire on the one hand and fusion of two souls on the other, love could be a source of misery or a source of delight according to the state of mind of its victims. Each protagonist was expected to support his contention with apposite quotations from the Classics.

Other Galley Commanders, from time to time, received the honor of an invitation to these theatrics, so it had not been difficult, by piecing together the program, to discover when it would fall to Augusto Contarini-Colonna to play a part, thus ensuring his certain absence from Venice. This had come about on the Saturday just passed, when he was cast in the role of paladin of the joys of love.

Returning to the Arsenale early on Monday morning he found his galley stripped of everything portable. The masts stood bare of rigging, his lovely canopy gone. In the hull remained little but the rowing benches. His cannon was still there, pointing down nakedly over the parapet, all ancillary equipment, swabs and tackles gone.

Augusto Contarini-Colonna raged through the other galleys like a madman howling vengeance and snatching wildly at items he thought were his. Someone brought this to the attention of the Provveditore. Officers were dispatched to detain him by force and lock him up pending investigation. Augusto then escaped, or more likely was allowed to escape by other officers. Related as he was to half the Golden Book he was determined to bring his influence to bear upon the Arsenale to reconstitute his galley as it was. He was detained, fuming in the antechamber of the Hall of the College, while Councilors unaware of his misfortune continued to debate Naval affairs at length. He exploded in fury when told by a secretary to return another day. He had half drawn his sword when, set upon by guards, he was borne down dark stairways and locked in one of the small prison cells under the Rio di Palazzo.

The Provveditore of the Navy went that afternoon to sound the opinion of the Palazzo Ducale. An inquiry was conducted, and Augusto Contarini-Colonna was released after giving a promise to behave himself. Instructions were given to arrest the perpetrators of the despoilment. Damage to a war galley at a time of severe danger to the Republic could be considered treason. It was decided that Augusto was to blame for his failure to ensure that his ship was properly guarded. In consequence of this event there followed an order from the Council of Ten that no Galley Commander or any officer under training was to leave Venice for the Terraferma while Venice was under threat from the Ottoman. Conscious of ridicule Augusto removed his denuded galley from the Arsenale and hid it in a little frequented creek.

This comical episode teaches me something that we in Capodistria never suspected; that a desperate shortage of ships and maritime supplies has somehow come about in this once great Sea Power. As we get up to leave the table I want to question Nicolò about this but he wanders into some thoughts of his own that he doesn't seem to want to share. He asks the others in which deserted creek the forlorn galley lies and hurries there. At least I suppose he is going there since he leaves, pausing only to tell me that I am expected at a reception at the Sanmichele house on the Rio Santa Maria Formosa Sunday evening. And so, notwithstanding the unsolicited intervention of this very intense cousin, in the end I am left to find my own feet.

CHAPTER SIX

"Over here with a flask and two goblets, Wine Steward!" shouts a cheery, dumpy officer. "Stay and sit down," he says to me, grasping me by the arm, "I'm from Verona - stranger to Venice same as you are. I overheard some of that. Now, let me tell you how to enjoy life in this city."

I imagine that my Capodistrian outlandishness intrigued him. And that evening over a flask of wine at the refectory table he feasted my eager ears with stories of his gallantries.

The following morning the Provveditore of the Navy, the one I had seen explaining things to the Doge, paints a different picture of the life I might expect as I sit facing him across a heavy table set under one of the windows of his huge office the walls of which are decorated with the trophies of victories won in the years before the Ottoman had gained maritime supremacy. He asks me the same question that Nicolò had asked. Why do I want to enter the Venetian Navy?

The most honest of us must admit that the answers we give often depend on the questioner. Seated before this august man in this time-honored setting I am inclined to present the more idealistic side of my nature and reply, not untruthfully, that I too thought to play a part in stemming the tide of barbarity that threatens to swamp Venice and all Europe if it is not brought to a halt. Glory in my boyhood indeed meant galleys and battles at sea: it meant the Great Galleon of Venice and her valiant stand against the Ottoman at Prevesa; or, much earlier, the day when Doge Dandolo, ninety-four and blind, was the first to leap ashore, leading the Crusaders into Constantinople. I know well that the Provveditore will not sympathize with me if I mention that the capture of exotic oriental cities might lead to pleasures of another kind.

Solemnly the Provveditore asks me if I fully understand what a commission in the Venetian Navy means. He explains;

"The exoneration an officer could once have claimed if the Venetian warship in which he was serving failed to bring the enemy to battle with a successful outcome is now in abeyance in consequence of a decree passed by the Senate following last year's reverses. This decree makes trial mandatory for delinquent officers. It is true that victory will still bring you honor and perhaps a share of the spoils, but defeat or misconduct will, under the new laws, make you liable to the harshest punishment and humiliation, which you will only escape if you are killed or captured. If you are captured, of course, you may face the long drawn out agony of dying under the lash on the rowing bench of an enemy war galley."

Misconduct? Can he be thinking of what the Rector meant when he lectured on misconduct? And what could I say? I could hardly just thank him for the information, say that I had changed my mind, and would now go back to Capo d'Istria. Confronted by such a situation one can only try to convince oneself that things may not be as bad as described. Perhaps the Provveditore thinks me an unsuitable candidate and is trying to discourage me by painting a gloomy picture? But this could scarcely have been so since he seems to be taking my silence for acceptance, or perhaps he gives me credit for higher principles than really are mine for he goes on;

"Ser Marcantonio Sanmichele in his capacity as one of the Savi ai Ordeni controlling the Navy spoke to me about you yesterday evening. He wants you sent to the Venetian Flagship to serve as one of Admiral Veniero's aides, as a Flag Lieutenant. Admiral Veniero, the Commander-in-Chief, is conducting operations against Ottoman raiding forces in the Southern Adriatic. He will be ordered by the Senate to proceed to Messina in Sicily, there to join the Allied Fleets under Don John of Austria. For the present you are to remain in the Capodistrian galley, which will exercise for a few days with the Venetian galleys being brought out of reserve. This force, a dozen galleys altogether, will then sail to reinforce Admiral Veniero's fleet."

"Ser Marcantonio Sanmichele has ordered that the Capodistrian galley, in which, as I say, you will remain for the present, must call at Ancona, Brindisi, and then Corfu, before rejoining the rest. At Messina you will transfer to Admiral Veniero's staff on board the Flagship, handing him a letter that I shall give you. Ser Marcantonio Sanmichele particularly wants the Capodistrian ship to call at Corfu in order to show the colonists what support Venice is receiving from small dependencies like Capo d'Istria since he feels it necessary to bolster the morale of that island. Corfu is very much in danger from the enemy."

The appointment to Admiral Veniero's staff is not quite the destiny I had vaunted for myself before leaving Capodistria. I tell him that I had hoped that Ser Marcantonio Sanmichele would have obtained for me the command of a galley. The Provveditore doesn't treat the remark with disdain as he might have done but looks at me gravely;

"It is true that the law whereby command could only be given to Venetian nobles has been rescinded but the fact is that we still have Venetian nobles as well as merchant captains whose claims to command cannot be fairly superseded."

He appears to think that this answer settles the matter satisfactorily and continues;

"As to a servant, you may have one in your quarters, but you are expected to pay for his victualling, as well your own of course."

I assure him that my father has placed adequate funds with his agent on the Riva degli Schiavoni to cover all my needs. In mentioning this agent it occurs to me to complain about the sequestration of my father's galleon and its cargo of stone by the high-handed young officer at the entrance to the Laguna.

"Secrecy regarding our defensive operations prevented our informing the Prefect of Capo d'Istria or other Venetian territories that we are fortifying the San Nicolò and Malamocca entrances. For this we must commandeer any suitable ships that come to Venice to block these points by sinking them there as necessary. The Signoria will have acquainted your father's agent with the procedure for obtaining compensation. I think that Ser Sanmichele himself is in touch with the agent."

The Provveditore rises from his chair and bows to me with ponderous formality, displaying a perfunctory respect inconsistent with his words. A servant, who appears seemingly out of the oak-paneled walls, holds open the door for me to leave.

In the days that follow we are taken through programs of instruction in coastal navigation, ship handling under sail and under oars, operation and maintenance of cannon and small arms, conservation of powder and ammunition, acquisition and distribution of victuals, and various other miscellaneous matters such as folding and stowage of sails and repair of oars. The lectures take place in the refectory. There follows training in boarding with a training galley as opponent, exercising with soldiery embarked, and instructions on the use of the ram, and sword fighting.

In conversation with Venetians in the Arsenale I begin to get a picture of my master to be, the ever-angry, unrelenting and exacting Venetian Naval Commander-in-Chief, Sebastiano Veniero, who seems to me to be as old as time it. I resolve to tell my uncle, Marcantonio Sanmichele, at the first opportunity, that I will serve in any position in the Venetian Navy other than as one of Veniero's aides, the duties of which I know nothing. In fact I realize at this point that I know very little of anything and that it is in my interest to devote myself to learning as much as possible of what the Venetians can teach me of galley warfare in such a short period.

The main objective is to deliver on board the enemy ship a complement of fighting men in the briefest time possible. The artillery and ram are there, the first hopefully to clear the enemy decks of men, the second to sink him with all hands as an alternative to boarding. Using the cannon to launch burning material with chain shot to set the enemy ship on fire is another form of attack. And we learn that the enemy is extremely adept in manufacturing what is known as 'Greek fire', the components of which are sulphur, niter, naphtha and asphalt, and whatever else they put in it to cause a ghastly blaze. We are to be on guard for 'fire ships' loaded with this deadly weapon, which was launched successfully at Prevesa, setting Venetian galleys on fire.

In our simulated battles arquebusiers are placed in the waist of the galley to break up any concentrations in the enemy ships with the intention of opposing our boarding parties. But these and the cannon are seen as the prelude to the main battle that is hand to hand fighting, preferably on board their ships rather than ours. Then there is the concept of employing many galleys as a single unit, marshalling them and deploying them to outmaneuver a roughly equivalent enemy force. There are many theories that cause lively argument over matters outside our power to remedy: for example, the Senate's recent decrees laying down shipbuilding specifications are held by some to be the cause of unnecessary deaths since the particularly light Venetian construction fails to compensate for the weight of the ram and cannon and too often cause the leeward oars to go under in gusting winds. This is when sail has to be used in conjunction with oars, and its disastrous result is to smash the oar looms into the rowers' bodies, breaking their rib cages. There are those who argue that men are being wantonly sacrificed to the Venetian ships' reputation for lightness and swiftness.

But I have to confess that my mind is not entirely preoccupied with galleys. In the evenings my Veronese friend constantly alludes to another, voluptuous, Venice the other side the high crenulated walls of the Arsenale, images that disturb my healthy sleep with vague desire. Then another thing that worries me is the extraordinary behavior of Murad.

It is dangerous to insult a man who has little to lose, a man such as Murad. A slave-master who has had his whip thrown overboard, a slave-master who was driven away from slave girls like a randy stray dog from pet bitches, will harbor resentment and may well find an opportunity to express it in the confusion that occurs at times in a war galley. It is no consolation to me that in both instances I have acted under del Tacco's instructions. The uncouth are incapable of making such nice distinctions, and del Tacco would hardly be a target for revenge. Custom affords the Galley Commander an invisible but hallowed shield denied to those who have no special position in a ship. For my own safety I constantly keep a watchful eye on Murad. What I begin to observe causes me far more concern than if I encountered open hostility, for this swarthy shambling stalwart is beginning to afflict me with what looks very much like devotion.

Murad's unwelcome homage first displayed itself while I was in the process of rigging an awning to keep the scorching sun off Hassan's back. Del Tacco thinks it wise to keep Hassan chained to a bench in case he tries to escape - but as things turned out it would have been better had he been allowed to do so. I was startled to find Murad beside me holding a knife. I backed away slowly and he slowly turned the handle towards me, indicating a trifle too slowly that the knife was intended to cut a jammed knot I was ineffectively trying to unravel. I have heard of the torturer's mind that alternates baleful sympathy with honest torment, but I think that it could hardly be this in Murad's case, since from that time he repeatedly appears from nowhere to assist me in the most undemanding physical tasks.

This devotion angers Osvaldo, who takes it upon himself to spy on Murad and pester me with reports that he imagines will discredit that character. Some of what he says makes me suspicious since amongst other things he tells me that he has seen Murad with Nicolò who has entered the Arsenale without coming to see me. And I should be happier without Osvaldo's report that he caught Murad demonstrating methods of strangulation to the rowers.

CHAPTER SEVEN

Sunday is here at last and I can be free from my preoccupation with Murad for a few hours. I am invited to the Sanmichele's in the evening. But the day's events get in train much earlier when, in the middle of the morning, my Veronese friend walks into my room and asks me to join him and others at a wine shop he knows in the Piazza San Marco, where there is also good food to be had.

Nicolò is with me when he comes, helping me choose a longer, more sombre, and according to him more fashionable doublet from amongst some that a tailor is proposing. Dressed in this, I throw my discarded clothes at him exuberantly, asking him to get rid of them for me, and I set off with the Veronese. Perhaps my cousin resented my abandoning him like that but I am beginning to find his presence oppressive. Leaving him in this way I feel avenged a little for his Venetian disdain at seeing my gaudy Capodistrian attire, disdain which admittedly had not been voiced but which I am certain must be felt.

My Veronese friend, his friends, and I sit at a table under the giant colonnade bordering the Piazza San Marco. The wine flows freely. Our conversation becomes bolder as the hours pass and many a Venetian young lady comes into our view, always escorted by father or brother and sometimes by the whole family. As the wine flasks empty the girls seemed more delectable, but never remotely attainable. Available though, for a price, are the big sisters offered by small boys, sometimes their brothers, and sometimes the small boys themselves. It is long past noon when the Veronese announces that he knows of a 'house', an exclusive one, where admission demands an introduction that he happens to be able to give. He suggests that we should all go there.

I am disappointed when the others support this suggestion only half-heartedly, for the sight of so many pretty girls - at least they look pretty to me who had gazed on Capodistrian rowers for more than a week - had been too potent. I am secretly afraid lest the knowledgeable Veronese might be dissuaded from the idea. I need not have feared for when his charm has failed to entice the others away from their wine and conversation he grasps my arm with all the familiarity I had engendered as an eager listener to his gallantries. We slide away in excited complicity.

Rapidly we make our way through narrow streets occasionally slashed by bars of golden sunlight. Canals and bridges appear in strange and dreamlike perspective in the heady wine fumes and when a friend of my schooldays at the Academy of St Marco suddenly appears before me on the top step of one of the bridges, I think it funny to see him wearing a solemn visage and priestly garb. My reaction is shameful and I blush at the recollection. I imagine that he is clowning and appal even the Venetian passers by in trying to drag him with us to the brothel, inadequately explaining to shocked onlookers that the priest was my school-friend. The young priest tears himself away and we hurry on our lecherous mission.

Soon we come to the Rio Santa Marina where a group of gondoliers stand gossiping against the bridge railing. With loosely clasped left hand and prodding right index finger the Veronese wordlessly conveys in sailors' language our objective, and a gondola carries us to the colonnaded steps of an elegant small palazzo. The Veronese knows it well and leads the way through the echoing hall just above canal level and up a staircase set in the thickness of the right hand wall all the time describing to me the merits of the girls to be obtained there.

We come to a room almost entirely furnished with damask-covered cushions of all sizes, on the wall a single painting, that of the Virgin Mary. As we enter an elegant lady, sweetly welcoming and groomed as for a cardinal's drawing room, comes towards us. The Veronese makes enthusiastic references to his former visits that she ignores completely. She claps her hands and a group of girls appear, naked and smiling: brunette Bedouins, redheaded Turks and blonde Italians. Raising my eyes I meet a warm blue gaze half-hidden by corn-coloured hair. I push aside a goblet of wine that a servant is trying to give me as ruthlessly as Hassan had done that night on the galley and grasp her arm to deny her to the Veronese. But he is not a contender; his interest lies elsewhere and the Madame promptly moves forward to demand my golden ducats.

In an adjacent bedroom I throw off the sombre doublet, struggle out of the intractable hose and tight boots in fashion. The girl lies back calmly on the sumptuous bed with unashamed abandon: Then, in the manner of ladies whose profession is to please men but are paradoxically unconcerned with the way this is done she launches herself at me and clings to me like a pet monkey in a shipwreck, moving so vigorously in all directions that I feared an injury to my person. I cannot make her desist since I have no communication with her. She has forced her head somewhere under my left shoulder and it is too late for me

She is gone. I drag on my clothes. I wonder whether to wait and see if the establishment cannot do better. The Veronese's commendations come back to me and I feel cheated. The decision is not left in my hands. I am the client of a machine. Thinking that I am being shown back into the cushiony reception room I allow a servant to usher me through a door that places me irrevocably outside in a quiet and narrow street. The Venetian Madame is well aware of the disastrous consequences that might ensue if entrance and egress were through the same portals and the organization is designed to avoid this. I wonder about the Veronese, and then decide that I have seen enough of him for one day.

In the melancholy hours that must pass before appearance at the Sanmicheles' house I wander dispiritedly in the direction of and then around the walls of my old school. Time passes and eventually I think I can go to Santa Maria Formosa. I come back across the Rio Santa Marina Bridge where two ancient citizens, high cloaked against recognition notwithstanding the warm weather, are being helped into a boat. What arrangements has the efficient Madame in hand for those who don't survive the Sunday afternoon athletic contest that none seem too old to participate in?

With time still in hand I make my way to Campo San Marino and come to Sanmichele's canal. I hang around the bridge hesitating to enter the Sanmichele palazzo. This, oddly enough, stands in exactly the same relationship to the bridge as does the Madame's house to the bridge on her canal.

Then I see gondola leave the palazzo steps and in it are two female figures. One is the elder Circassion girl dressed in black and improbably holding on her lap a large Missal. The other slender figure is completely veiled, but I assume that it is the Sanmichele daughter,

Nicolò's sister and gather from the booming of the great bell of Santa Maria Formosa behind me that she is going to Benediction. The slave girl waves. When I cross the bridge to the other railing to see the boat emerge from under I hear a soft admonition. Both look down as they come to the church steps where they land.

CHAPTER EIGHT

I decide to enter the Sanmichele house from the garden entrance in a little side street. This gives immediate access to the entrance hall of the living quarters. Iron bonded chests decorated with allegoric paintings lie against the walls of the entrance hall and the black and white marble chequered floor is bare of carpet. I know that the two arched openings in the right hand wall give access through curtains to Marcantonio Sanmichele's library. This I remember from my schoolboy visits since it was there that I was taken to be admonished by him.

As I enter black robed guests are arriving by the stairway approach from canal level below, and my uncle is standing near the head of the staircase to receive them, accompanied by that paragon of virtue, Monsignor Paolo Loredan, the Rector of San Marco, and his son also named Paolo, a year younger than me, who was my greatest enemy at school. It is simply that we hate each other instinctively. I see that he has grown into an excessively tall, skinny, yellow-faced man. He is now, he tells me, an officer in one of the galleys.

There is another disquieting figure, a very tall, muscular Dominican Friar with a completely bald head set awry on a scraggy neck, whose piercing glance, like that of a curious and disdainful bird, evaluates all it falls upon only to deprecate all. He leans forward, allowing a heavy staff to take his weight, and his wooden crucifix swings freely before his black cassock. Strangely he immediately turns to examine me while I try to distance myself from these grave arrivals. Sanmichele, seeing his gaze switch from himself to my person, notices me for the first time and presents me to the Dominican, whom he introduces as Ludovico Priuli. Priuli's ardent eyes moved up and down my body and I grow uncomfortable and awkwardly disengage myself from his company.

Cesare, the old steward, gives me an excuse to get away from him. Cesare is serving Marsala:

"Ah! It must be the Signorino Marco Valente! A handsome young lord he has become indeed."

But neither the Marsala nor the conversation of the guests can do anything to lighten my spirits, excessively low as sickness replaces the intoxicating effect of the lunchtime wine. Around me Senators and Ambassadors are deploring the state of trade with the East, the ravages of the Muslims, the failure to relieve Farmagosta, their dark cloaks and nodding shapeless velvet hats attesting to the gravity of their statements. I feel hungry and follow Cesare into his pantry, familiar from boyhood memories. He hurriedly hides some package he was holding behind some casks and turns to me, bowing ingratiatingly.

"When are we going to eat?" I ask him, "I'm hungry."

"We shall dine very soon, and well, from roast duck brought to us from Noventa by the Signorina Michaela."

He grasps my arm his face too close to mine. Do I remember the pretty Michaela? His tongue protrudes wetly between his thick lips and he makes a half sucking, half smacking show of relish, not for the duck but for the girl.

"The signorina has grown into a lovely peach."

I push him away from me and he starts to get out crockery, sensually grunting Michaela's attributes to himself. I feel in no mood to rejoin the pontificating politicians around the Sanmicheles and go through them into the salone and out onto the balcony overlooking the canal. It is that time of evening when, the end of a serene summer's day, a pinky-golden haze enfolds the marble facades of Venetian palaces almost as palpably as the water laps at their foundations. I am lulled into reverie by the devitalized murmur that reaches me from inside. Darkness begins to fall. I look back through the window to see Cesare and a woman servant dragging a heavy dining table into the centre of the salone, then chairs, then Cesare is lighting the candelabra. The woman servant brings in dishes and puts them on the table. Then a slim, pretty, girl with golden hair falling wavily over her shoulders walks into the room and helps herself to some delicacies from the dishes.

Michaela Sanmichele must have walked into many rooms before without affecting others as she now affects me, causing me to gasp at her perfection. Shyness overcomes me and I shrink from re-entering the salone from the dusk outside. Then I see the Dominican, Priuli, come into the room. I think he will talk to Michaela but to my surprise he ignores her and, crossing over to the balcony window, comes out and to join me.

"You didn't give me the chance to say how welcome you are to Venice, Signorino Valente."

He takes my left hand in his right far too familiarly given our hardly existing acquaintanceship. Glancing through the window, I see the Sanmichele family come into the salone with Monsignor Loredan and the gangling Paolo. Priuli sees them too and obviously feels the need to speed up what he has to say. He bends his vulturous head close to my cheek;

"Love is what I have to offer, Marco, my darling," and so saying he drops my hand and makes to stroke my buttock. I whip out my dagger, but even as I make the movement the thought that he is a Man of God makes me suspend the stroke within an inch of his ribs. He takes a step back in fright, exposing a sandal, peeping out from under his soutane. As I sheath the dagger I step hard on this. He yelps and grabs the balcony rail, holding his foot up in pain.

"You have insulted the wrong person!" he hisses, and goes limping into the room. I follow, and feel myself blushing, not knowing where to look. The Sanmichele family are pretending to see nothing strange in our entrance from the balcony. Perhaps Priuli's predilections come as no surprise to them. But why have I overreacted and inflicted a painful assault on the monk? I think a combination of two things made me momentarily lose control of myself. Priuli's unwelcome advances jerked me into realization that my new role as galley officer had done nothing to alter my slender figure and what others in Capodistria had called my immature appearance, and Priuli's amorous advances seemed to confirm this at the very moment when I desperately needed to see myself as a muscular older male such as I imagined Michaela Sanmichele would admire.

Priuli is stumbling out of the salone. Nicolò is shouting at Cesare,

"Where is the wine, DOG?" Raising his arm threateningly at Cesare.

Cesare turns to him with a gap toothed grin and slinks away to his pantry. Marcantonio Sanmichele is addressing his son,

"Let's stop ill treating him," says he wearily.

We all sit around the table, and there follows one of those lulls in conversation that tend to occur when strangers have left, appetite prickles, and the transition has not yet been made from the courteous exchanges of polite society to candid pronouncements upon departed visitors. Monsignor Loredan fills the awkward gap with inquiries into my academic progress. As quondam pupils tend to do, I parry and slide past what I know is significant to him and expand, too well, on revolutionary thinking, to the gaping astonishment of the younger Loredan.

The Tridentine Index of 1564 has permitted many new versions of Classical texts to come off the printing presses. My father has no regard for, or even comprehension of, the peril of departing from conventional thinking, and has stocked our library in Capo d'Istria with every new publication brought to his attention. Thus it is that from the texts of such as Homer, Hesiod and Strabo, I have elaborated what seemed to me a brilliant theory; that at some point around the eighth or seventh century before the Christian era the Earth had come close to destruction when the planets Mars and Venus were in conflict, as described by Homer in metaphorical terms.

With peasant Capodistrian disregard for the danger of expressing such unorthodox ideas in sophisticated society, carried away by what I was sure was admiration in the girl's eyes, I sketch for them my idea of well developed civilizations cataclysmically and convulsively burnt up, and the confounding terror of noise and universal fire. I point out the vast importance that the Ancients placed on this awful catastrophe, such as the deification of Mars by the Romans; and how the balance of the globe was so upset that a new celestial north came into place, a north star no longer contained in the seven bright stars of the Wagon, as Calypso suggests in her navigational advice to Ulysses. I am saying altogether too much about many things, including the geology of Istria and orientation of temples.

Nicolò's reaction to my various theories is less flattering than his sister's. His eyes keep wandering to the door. Sanmichele himself is immersed in thoughts of his own and goes to and fro between the salone and his library looking increasingly troubled. I realize that the Sanmichele males feel that they have fully met a polite obligation to listen for a few minutes to a visiting kinsman and I suddenly cease my monologue.

"Are you interested in architecture, Signorino Marco?" inquires Michaela sweetly.

People usually ask such questions as a pretext for introducing their own opinion on a subject of their choice. How happy I shall be to hear her opinion on anything!

"He is interested in architecture only in so far as it uses up stone!" interposed the sarcastic younger Paolo.

"You must see San Giorgio Maggiore," continues Michaela as though unaware of the interruption, "which is near where you anchored while waiting to be called by the Doge? Much remains unfinished, but the flow of light and color in the chancel.........."

"All these fine phrases!" interrupts Sanmichele dryly. "She must have prepared them for you," he adds before leaving once more on one of his excursions, looking hard at Michaela who blushes and casts her eyes downwards. Nevertheless she turns to Loredan when her father leaves:

"Monsignor, Signorino Marco must give a talk at the Academy on the ideas he has derived from reading Classical texts. You are always looking for ex-students to give talks." She holds out her hands to the Rector in a winsome, pleading gesture. The Rector is looking extremely uncomfortable.

"Michaela, I hardly think this......."

He is relieved of the requirement to put his objections into words by Senator Sanmichele's startled reappearance. Michaela puts her hands to her lips, her eyes wide with fear, and rushes to him. Sanmichele has information for them apparently about Priuli;

"He'll be returning to his Convent on San Stefano Island. His boat will leave from the outer end of the Canareggio where Contarini-Colonna has hidden his despoiled galley. It is better done tonight. It would be too dangerous to wait until tomorrow. Make sure nothing is said."

"How can he say anything?" Nicolò demands sternly.

Sanmichele looks at him in astonishment.

"You aren't using Murad for this? If he fails the victim will be able to say it was one of us"

"Then I'll do the job myself, and I won't fail," says Nicolo, "but I've sent him on."

"Make sure nobody recognizes you, and get Murad back!"

"I told him to follow Priuli and.........."

"Get him back!"

Naturally I am being ignored in this family interchange, but now Nicolo looks at me or rather at my clothes, then he glances away quickly as my eyes catch his. He is leaving the room, but not the house, for I hear him saying something to Cesare as I take my leave of the family.

"May it please God it's not traced to us!" Says Michaela as she holds out her hand absently for my parting kiss. The younger Loredan tries to hang back to speak to her, but the Sanmicheles no longer have any interest in their supper guests and we make our way out without further formalities. The Loredans go down to the canal entrance where I suppose a gondola is waiting for them, and I am go to the door leading out to the little side street so like the Madam's exit.

CHAPTER NINE

On Monday the ship's routine obligations again face me but in a transformed world. The enchantment that lays the other side the shipyard walls is no longer only for others but can also be mine. For me there is now Michaela Sanmichele, and while I go happily about my tasks in the ship I think up schemes whereby I might get to know her better. As a man wants to know a girl yes, but much more than that. A lonely child imagines a mate with whom he can share his thoughts, and who thinks like him. Perhaps when he grows older he finds a girl who attracts him physically and desire blinds him to the reality that she doesn't think like him at all and never will. All he knows is the image he has created in his own mind. But for the moment he believes he has found his soul mate. And I have found Michaela.

Another reason for contentment is the absence of Murad. Ordinarily, in his newfound and perplexing devotion, he would be running before me opening up hatchways and clearing men out of my path. Even Osvaldo comments on his disappearance when he comes to tell me that Domenico del Tacco asking for me. I went to him;

"Have you seen Augusto Contarini-Colonna? He should have come to talk to me regarding arrangements for tomorrow," demanded Domenico.

"Tomorrow?"

"Yes, we sail tomorrow for Fasana, not far. This is a brief cruise to see what we have learnt during our week's training. We sail with the Venetian galleys that are training with us. They have given the command of this squadron to Contarini-Colonna, and since his galley is laid up in some creek he will exercise temporary command of the squadron from this ship, the Leona, but I shall remain in command of the ship, of course."

"So we have to sail?"

"Of course we have to sail if we are going to cross the Adriatic to Fasana. Before dawn, too."

I sense from Domenico's attitude that I had better appear helpful. Accordingly I go and look for Augusto Contarini-Colonna, although to tell the truth the news that we are sailing so shocks me that I am anything but enthusiastic. I recruit Osvaldo in the search, and we meet up again in the refectory after half an hour, with no luck. However, Osvaldo reports that he had seen Nicolo. This is pleasant news for me since it means I'll have a chance to make contact with his sister. But I am fearful that Osvaldo has confused him with one of the many leather-jerkined, steel helmeted young men that roam the Arsenale since Osvaldo admits that he had only seen him from a distance in a boat.

However, going below I find Nicolo has sneaked on board and is impatiently waiting for me in my cabin. He seems to be in a highly agitated state, unable to stand still or sit still for two minutes on end. Breathlessly he informs me;

"My father sends me to talk to you. You must have guessed from our conversation yesterday evening what we were doing?"

"I have no idea what you were doing," not admitting that I was nevertheless curious.

"My father has not slept all night in case, not knowing the true circumstances, you should reveal to someone what you heard. There are many things that must be explained to you. To begin, what do you know of the Holy Inquisition?"

"What do Capodistrians know of the Holy Inquisition?" I shout, annoyed at the arrogant tone of Nicolo's speech. "We know of the horrid and long drawn out death of the Capodistrian, Lupetina, at your Venetian hands; slow torture below the Doge's Palace in a cell flooded once a day to the point of nearly drowning him. Then when they finally realized that he would not recant, beheading him at your sacred place of execution between the columns of the Piazzetta."

"He was not beheaded," asserts Nicolò "but simply drowned on the orders of the Doge as an act of clemency. Had the Signoria acted as the Holy Office wanted he would have been burnt alive. Venice has saved others from the fire in spite of the Dominican."

The strong morning light streaming into my cabin through the latticed windows, the cheerful sound of hammering and sawing and the banter of the zestful shipyard workers, all contrasted oddly with this gloomy conversation.

"The Dominican!* you mean Priuli?" Here is something to interest me after what happened between him and me on the Sanmicheles' balcony. "What IS he then?"

"He was the Roman Inquisitor, sent to intensify the campaign......"

"Was?"

"Well, ostensibly he was here to assist, as the representative of the Holy Office, in drafting the many amendments which Venice insisted on making to the Holy League Treaty."

"I see. So he's going?"

"Have patience, Marco," he pleads, "and I will explain everything. Let me begin this way: my friends and I form a political society. We are called 'I Giovanni', the Young, and we are called this disparagingly by the Signoria and the Elders. We are dedicated to keeping Venice free from the terror of the Holy Inquisition, this Roman insult to our Republic. We need your help."

"I have already told you the answer to that. My father's instructions to me on leaving Capodistria were that I am not to involve myself in Venetian politics."

"This is not Venetian politics; it is my family, we, your cousins, need your help. First let me give you the background to the situation."

He had prepared himself well and I admit that my interest was kindled when he strove to convince me that now any slight divergence in thought, any philosophical pronouncement, even a slip of the tongue, anything that could be imagined as remotely antagonistic to the orthodox body of opinion, itself uncertain, could lead to torture. Torture could be stretching on the rack until the blood gushed from the mouth, or branding with hot irons. The freedom of thought that the 'Giovanni' were fighting for went a good deal further than freedom to make heretical statements about Christian dogma.

Particularly horrible are the contents of some documents he reads out to me: they were the routine reports of a religious organization called 'The Comforters,' and they describe what the 'comforting' consists in. When a tortured victim, cursed with a constitution that condemns him to continue to live through hideous torture, has finally confessed and is left in peace to await death by burning the 'Comforters' are ordered by the Court of Inquisition to proceed to his cell. There they group around him and fill his last hours reciting prayers and chanting, making sure that wherever his fatigued gaze rests he will see the symbols of the dogma he couldn't accept even in his agony. The Comforters unrelentingly tempt him with the happy alternative of death by strangulation if only he will recant.

"That's Rome!" says Nicolò, "And the Holy Office in that city announces that it is scandalized by the failure of the Venetian Senate to curb the heretical activities of German, French, and English students at the University of Padova, which is a Venetian responsibility. The Holy office is also appalled by Venice's lack of enthusiasm in preventing large consignments of arms being sent from the Venetian province of Brescia to the French Protestants."

"Why should Venice want to send arms to the French?" I inquire, perhaps irrelevantly, but suspecting that I am being led back into Venetian politics in spite of what I keep telling him.

"Well, never mind about that," he turns away impatiently. "It is not important to us. What is important is my father's position now that the Treaty called the Holy League has been ratified."

At that point Osvaldo comes creeping into the cabin to tell me that Augusto Contarini-Colonna is on board, and in the Galley Commander's quarters, should I wish to see him. Osvaldo remembers that I have mentioned that I would like to talk to Contarini-Colonna about stellar navigation. Before I can reply Nicolò puts his arm around my shoulders;

"Contarini-Colonna doesn't matter now," he whispers persuasively. "You have months ahead in which to talk to him. Come, I want to show you where our society meets, and introduce you to some of the others."

I go, but my motive for accompanying him doesn't match his politico-religious fervor, and this soon becomes apparent to him from my line of conversation as we pick our way through the shipyard around huge coils of rope and over planks, avoiding the heat of the forges.

"Is Loredan's son, Paolo, a close friend of ... of your family?" I ask.

"The Loredans have no money," is Nicolo's answer, which shows that he somehow senses where my interest lies.

"Will your sister remain in Venice or return to live with her mother at Noventa?"

I feel he is angry only because I am not showing more feeling for his cause against the Inquisition. At that point I can't know how painful is the family matter that possesses his mind. He decides after a little time to answer me.

"Your cousin, Michaela, should have remained with our mother at Noventa all along". The 'cousin' seems to me rather pointedly designed to emphasize our close family ties, "but she is so distressed that she insists on being in Venice because she thinks she can help us."

He doesn't explain why she is so distressed and we walk on in silence for a little while;

"Michaela should stay there. Venice is no place for a young girl whose father cannot hope to compete with richer patrician families in the matter of a dowry, not unless she is to be wasted on some ancient widower. We Sanmicheles haven't the money to dress or entertain properly. That's why my mother stays at Noventa. Then there's that swine, Cesare!"

We arrive at the north-west corner of the battlements surrounding the Arsenale, and entering we find a long, high vaulted, candlelit area stacked on either side with demijohns. Nicolò leads the way through a hole in the far wall and up a spiral staircase into a long narrow room that must be contained in the thickness of the outer curtain wall of the Arsenale. At the far end several young men are seated around a table with decanters and glasses. Nicolò presents me to them. I notice among them the arrogant young man that boarded us on the morning we arrived from Capodistria. Nicolò then takes me to a table well away from them. We sit for a while. Perhaps he is debating with himself whether it would be useful, useful to the Sanmicheles that is, to tell me about Cesare and Michaela. Evidently he decides that it might serve;

"What happened with Cesare happened a few months ago in the early summer; that is when I caught him though there might have been other occasions. It was partly Michaela's fault since from the time she was little she was in the habit of lying naked on her bed in the heat of the afternoon. I was in my room, and my father was at the Signoria as usual. Cesare was wandering around the house, tidying up, and Michaela never troubled to lock her bedroom door or even close it. She was half asleep when Cesare went in. He crossed her room to the window, playing with it for a while. Then suddenly he was on her bed, pleading with her, and putting his hand on her. She leapt up screaming, and wrapping herself in a sheet, ran into my room."

"Before I could get him Cesare locked himself in his pantry. I waited with a heavy leather belt, and eventually he stumbled out, breathless. I forced him over the edge of the dining table and thrashed him so that he couldn't walk properly for days. His gnarled and hairy hindquarters revolted me, more like an old goat, which he is."

Hot anger sweeps through me. I didn't see that some of the fault lay with the girl for innocently hardening the old servant's desire to the point that he exposed himself to hideous punishment, rendered helpless through lust from preventing his horny hands from fondling a patrician girl.

"He must go!" I declare, banging the table with my hand, which brings curious glances from the other tables. Nicolò is surprised at the intensity of my feelings.

"He cannot go, as things stand at the moment."

"Why?"

"Better not talk here any more," he whispers.

So even here, inside the Republic's fortifications, among Nicolo's own military colleagues, it is not safe to talk about whatever distresses the San Michele family.

CHAPTER TEN

Nicolò leads the way up a continuation of the same spiral stairway until we come out onto the sentry walk along the battlements of the Arsenale, where the wind disperses our voices into the void.

"First you must swear an oath," demands Nicolò, "upon this Missal which I found in my father's library and which once belonged to his sister, you dear dead mother. Look inside the cover."

I open it and there in the round childish script of long ago is my mother's name, Caterina Valente.

"Why should you want on oath from me, Nicolò? I will not betray your interests. In any case I shall be gone soon."

"It will be even more important when you have gone"

"How?"

He evades a direct answer, replying;

"Any man, you included, may be put under intolerable pressures, where loyalties break down. If you are loyal to us you cannot object to swearing. Simply say 'I swear on this my dear mother's Missal and before God to defend the Sanmicheles with all the means in my power and never to betray their interests.' "

"All right" I swear on this my dear mother's missal and before God to defend the Sanmicheles with all the means in my power and never to betray their interests."

As I say 'Sanmicheles' am thinking mainly of Michaela Sanmichele.

"Perhaps you would like to keep the Missal?"

"Thank you."

It is strange that Missal was so sacred to us, when in another context it would have been symbolic of the very Inquisitional terror he was fighting.

"Priuli was killed last night," he declares.

I ask him to repeat this because I seem to have heard wrongly. He repeats the words.

"Why did you have to murder Priuli?" my words slip out.

"Did I say I murdered him?"

I stay silent and he ponders for a while:

"Let us say Priuli had to be killed because Cesare had stolen, and given him letters from the French to my father. Cesare took them from my father's library. My father was reluctant to keep such correspondence at the Signoria, and was careless at home. Cesare must have put himself at Priuli's disposal for such services in revenge for my beating. We don't know what else he might have taken from the library and hidden somewhere. For this reason my father won't throw Cesare out. But Priuli had to die."

When I made no comment he went on, in self-justification, I suppose;

"You probably wonder how Priuli came to frequent our house? Well, my father at first encouraged his visits since he thought it expedient to cultivate a rapport with him. Priuli is a friend of Cardinal Granville, the Spanish Ambassador at Rome. My father hoped to get some exploitable information regarding the nefarious intentions of Spain that might support his pro-French policy in the Senate. The King of France has shown himself favorable to a separate treaty of peace between Venice and the Ottomans which would allow Venetian trade to flourish again in the East. At the same time it would save Venice the vast expense of building and equipping war galleys and the cost of maintaining fortresses in Dalmatia, the Peloponnese, the Aegean islands, Crete and Cyprus; expenses which the Senate cannot afford any longer."

"At the beginning of this year, Jacopo Ragazzoni, the Secretary of the Senate, was sent to Istanbul to discover Turkish intentions in this direction. Meanwhile my father and the proponents of the pact with the Muslims used every tactic available to them to delay the signing of the Holy League Treaty that Spain sought to impose. Trivial amendments were suggested by Venice as pretexts for the continued delay. In Rome the Holy See perceived these tactics and sent Priuli to counter this scheme. But Ragazzoni has taken far too long, and now any move towards a pact with the Ottomans is balked by a clause in the Holy League Treaty, now signed, which explicitly forbids the Allies to enter into separate treaties. This leaves my father and his friends at the mercy of the Spanish sympathizers in our Senate and of course the Holy Office. It was in an effort to enhance his political status that my father organized the Doge's ceremonial welcome for the Capodistrian galley."

"The Spanish sympathizers have another string to their bow as a result of this Holy League Treaty. The French Ambassador and French envoys with whom my father has treated are renowned heretics, and this association makes the Sanmicheles liable to trial and imprisonment by the Holy Inquisition."

So that is it!

"You must get Michaela away from Venice immediately," I announce, shocked at the fate she would surely suffer.

"Michaela!" he laughed. "Michaela will be arrested for heresy the day they desanctify the Holy Virgin."

He is quiet for a while. Perhaps it was then that it occurred to him that the potential threat to Michaela might be a useful tool in getting my collaboration,

"It is true that she would be in danger if my father were imprisoned or executed, and this might happen if the Ambassador Soranzo in Rome sent back to the Council of Ten a report on his negotiations with the French. This would certainly have happened if Priuli had been left to return to Rome with Alphonse Didier's letter. That is why ...."

"Alphonse Didier? But that's my father's agent who has his office on the Riva degli Schiavoni! What has he got to do with it?"

Nicolò steps back at my angry bark and I catch his arm as he comes too close to the unparapeted inner wall of the battlements.

"This has nothing to do with your father, Marco."

"How could it? He would not get involved in such a mess."

"He doesn't need to. He is rich," says Nicolò bitterly. "In any case, Didier is an agent for many things."

"So I imagine!"

At last it comes out, so painfully that I it arouses my sorrow for Nicolò as he turns away and relates to the stones how, in the previous April, his father has accepted twenty thousand ducats from the French, with the mediation of Didier, in recompense for his undertaking to delay, under whatsoever pretext, Venetian signature to the Holy League Treaty pending the outcome of Ragazzoni's mission to Istanbul, and how some of the correspondence must have got into Priuli's hands.

It seems that Priuli at first threatened to denounce the Senator by bringing the matter to the attention of the Venetian Ambassador to the Holy See, who by the very nature of his office was an enemy of the pro-French faction. The family lived for weeks in fear of Marcantonio Sanmichele's imprisonment and death. Then one Sunday evening Priuli told them, to everyone's astonishment, that what he really wanted was Michaela. He wanted her to go into the Convent founded by his order, the Dominicans, on the nearby Laguna island of San Stefano, where they care for poor girls.

"But Priuli........?"

"He didn't want her as a girl. You must know that!"

I feel my face reddening.

"What does he want then?"

"He wanted her as a hostage. By denouncing my father he could gain nothing. By holding the threat of denunciation over him, he could make my father work for him, and meanwhile he wanted Michaela as a living pledge."

This appalling explanation left me speechless. I think it was an attempt to bring the conversation back to normality that prompted Nicolò to say after a while;

"The Rector was interested in the theories you have formed from reading the Classics. Michaela will help you to prepare a paper for the Academy if you wish."

I confess that I had failed to notice the Rector's interest, and am astonished that he thinks Michaela can help in an undertaking of that kind. Also it began to dawn upon me that my theories were better kept to myself since there could be other reptilian clerics like Priuli in Venice. But I could not resist this heaven sent chance to be alone with Michaela.

"There is little time before finally sailing," I pretend to hesitate.

"Little time," says he. "When do you return to Venice from the exercise you are leaving for tomorrow?"

"The day after tomorrow - we shall be away one night - if the squadron doesn't meet any Muslims! Then in a day or so we finally leave."

"Little time," repeats he laconically. Then after some reflection he adds, "I'll send you a message telling you when to come. Your best way back to the galley, although not the quickest, is to follow around the inside of the Arsenale wall."

CHAPTER ELEVEN

Nicolò has not sent a message. He arrives in person to tell me to be at the Sanmichele house that same evening, and to bring any texts so that Michaela and I can work together on what we are supposed to prepare for the Rector and the Academy. By now I have learnt enough of the danger of expressing my thoughts to dismiss any idea of presenting my theories at the Academy. But I can't refrain from accepting this scholarly assignment with Michaela; more delicious than I ever dreamt would come my way.

But I have a question for Nicolò;

"What have you done with the clothes you offered to throw away for me on Sunday morning?"

"I threw them away, as you told me."

"Where?"

"Well I gave them to Cesare to throw away. Don't ask me what he did with them."

"Murad brought that green doublet on board when he returned from I don't know where:"

"Grazie al Dio!" exclaimed Nicolò, "then it won't fall into the hands of the Guardia della Notte."

"But if it does fall into the hands of the Guardia della Notte it won't be too difficult to trace it to me and arrest me for assaulting Priuli. At least one of the Guardia who came on board when we arrived will recognize that unfortunate doublet."

"If that happens my father can see that it is suppressed Nicolò", he replied uncertainly.

"You know Priuli's not dead, of course. He's on Augusto Contarini-Colonna's galley."

"So that's where he went."

"Did you murder him?"

"Marco! Was murder so far from your own thoughts?" he retorts mockingly. "Remember, you yourself had your dagger within an inch of his heart that same evening." Then, seconds later, he adds, "Murad must have gone back when I left the scene. It was very, very dark at the end of that canal."

I am still new to Venice and very unsure of my ground. If it was he who made the onslaught it was unlikely that he would admit it to me, and if he did admit it? I was in no position to call his colleagues to arrest him, and I didn't know whom else I might call. I could hardly tell my commanding officer Domenico del Tacco that I think my cousin is guilty of trying to kill a monk. It won't help me to have him think that my illustrious uncle houses an assassin. Indeed I realize that if I report it to anybody and the allegation is taken seriously I shall be removed from the ship and held prisoner while the thing is investigated, in which case del Tacco will be bound to get to know. If I am held will I ever be released to give evidence aimed at convicting a Senator's son? There is no alternative to keeping quiet.

When I arrive at the canal steps that evening there is only the Sanmicheles' gondolier to greet me. The palazzo seems deserted as I climb the stairs and enter the salone. Michaela comes out from hiding, tiptoeing behind me, laughingly taking me by surprise. She is barefoot in a loose gown, and barely comes up to my shoulder. Avoiding formalities she runs out and comes back with writing paper and materials. The elder Circassian girl comes in with a tray loaded with cold meats and wine and starts to serve us, but Michaela tells her that she is not required. The girl leaves, tossing her head.

We eat and drink, shyly avoiding each other's glances. My excuse for being there, those theories, seems to be increasingly odd and unapproachable. She has no such reservations. She unconcernedly clears the plates away and lays our equipment out on a side table.

"You have only brought this one, Signorino Marco?"

I have been careful to limit my contribution to an extract of Hesiod's works, which describes the misery of his world in such general terms that it might have applied to any period in history.

"My apologies, Signorina Michaela, but you may imagine that I cannot take many books in that galley."

"Never mind - we have enough."

We drag up two huge carved armchairs to the table and laugh when we find that although they touch each other we are still too far apart to look over the same page together. So we drag up a chest to sit on at the table.

"It is too hard!" she says, and runs off upstairs to come down stumbling under an armful of cushions.

We settle on these, and I read out to her a piece of Hesiod, to which she listens submissively but disconcertingly since her eyes are on me rather than on the text. I ask her to make some notes that, dutifully, she does. The summer evening slowly fades and reflections from the canal, now crossing the white ceiling, become rosier. The banter of gondoliers, coming only distantly into the room, emphasizes our isolation from the outside world. She re-arranges herself, loses her balance, and I have to save her from toppling backwards.

"There is great trouble for my family now, Marco," Is she pretending that she hasn't noticed that I am holding her? "Nicolò bungled things and Priuli is still alive."

"Nicolò?" question I casually, hoping not to break the spell that had brought Michaela into my arms, not understanding that the girl is beside herself with terror for her father's life and for herself, now that the dangerous Dominican is back amongst them, his malignancy augmented tenfold by the Sanmicheles' criminal attempt on his life.

Subdued girlish giggles from somewhere greet my inane 'Nicolò?' and I detect a movement behind one of the large curtains. I leap up and tear it back to reveal Cesare and the two slave girls. Cesare, fearing a thrashing for seeking to enjoy vicariously what he was agonizing to do with Michaela, lopes off fast to his pantry; and of course the girls run away, laughing helplessly. Michaela is now on her feet, leaning over the table and sobbing. I try to comfort her, but she picks up my Hesiod and hurls it at me with unexpected force. I hurriedly leave the Sanmichele house. When I arrive back in the Arsenale I go straight to my bedroom above the refectory, but I am too restless to sleep. Although not shackled to a rowing bench, I am as effectively barred from slaking my desire as was Hassan from possessing the slave girl in the galley. I spend much of the night leaning out of the window watching the disdainful moon's slow climb above the campaniles, each of which, near and distant, periodically intones its idiosyncratic assessment of the hour. All seems still amongst the phantom like galleys moored along the moon washed wharves below, except that peering more intently one can detect fleeting shadows; thieves? cats? assassins? The Sanmicheles had so contrived things that two would-be assassins wandered by the Canareggio on Sunday night and the intended victim, Priuli, in full knowledge of this attempt was still alive. A wounded snake.

I feel myself a beast. Instead of offering to help the maiden I am still intent on seducing her. I determine to find some way of clearing myself. But how, since I can no longer approach the Sanmichele house openly? I fear the morning and the wrathful father. Servants cannot hold their tongues and I no longer feel safe on Venetian territory.

CHAPTER TWELVE

There is hardly a hint of light in the eastern sky, and Venice astern of us remains cloaked in darkness. As often happens in summer, the wind has fallen in the night and the water is still and smooth, the ship sliding towards the dawn under the steady beat of the drum. We lie last in a line of five galleys, the others vaguely silhouetted ahead.

As the scheming city of Venice recedes into the dim west grey dawn turns through imperceptible stages into dazzling gold above the now clearly defined curve of the eastern horizon. A dolphin family arrives to play, and the parents and the little ones leap together for joy in the galley's bow wave. The clear notes of the trumpeter calling the arquebusiers to their stations ring through the crisp morning air.

While peering over the stern I can make out the shape of a sixth galley emerging from the Laguna entrance. "It's Contarini-Colonna," announces del Tacco who has been waiting for me to see this, and he clearly gets some satisfaction out of my surprise. I suspect that he is slightly envious, with very little reason, of my easy friendship with people like Contarini-Colonna. It seems that Contarini-Colonna has collected supplies together in that abandoned creek and equipped his galley for sea again. Not difficult, I suppose, with money and friends in the right places.

I am disappointed. He will not now be taking command of the squadron from Leona. I was looking forward to having him on board our galley to talk about stellar navigation and we could have taken the sun's declination together at noon with my quadrant. Augusto is interested in everything. This I discovered in talking to him in the refectory. We have since discussed drawing up a simple set of instructions for obtaining latitude with the quadrant, something that could free Galley Commanders from reliance on the lore of Sailing Masters. The authority of those in command is to some extent subverted since Sailing Masters and many veteran seamen seem to have an uncanny knowledge of their ship's position at sea even when days out of sight of land. This they gain from close attention to winds and currents, birds and fish, and simple dead reckoning through intuitive awareness of the distance covered. They deride navigation by the stars except in the crudest sense of watching where the Constellations lie.

Contarini-Colonna splits the squadron into two groups. The Tramontana comes up and we hoist the sails. Then, commanded by a simple flag signalling system first one group lowers sail, comes under oars, and simulates ramming; then the ships in this group become targets for ramming by the other group. Ramming under sail is unsatisfactory due the unmanageability of the galleys in getting the ram placed at right angles to the target ship, since the wind keeps bearing the bows away. Now we are exercising firing the cannon, which causes Domenico to think that it needs some elevation. The soldiery carry out boarding exercises, not very successfully since they cannot be prevailed upon to stage a lively attack while at the same time restraining themselves from inflicting real damage upon their fellows.

Towards midday a blue flag is hoisted at the fore peak of Augusto Contarini-Colonna's galley, the prearranged signal to terminate the exercises and allow the men to eat and rest. A boat comes from Augusto with invitations for Domenico del Tacco and me to dine on board his galley. Other Galley Commanders and their officers are similarly invited to Augusto's ship.

As we came near Augusto's galley we see that she is sadly shorn of any former gorgeousness, except for the magnificent Quarterdeck canopy, emblazoned in red and gold with the Contarini-Colonna crest, which Augusto himself found abandoned in a timber heap when he went prowling. We settle thankfully under its shade for the wind has dropped. There is barely enough breeze to lift the sails and the June sun blazes in a cloudless sky. We drift slowly towards the verdant Istrian coast, blue mountain backed.

I am in the midst of a conversation with someone whose eyes turn sharply away from me. I follow his gaze and see the horrid deathlike face of Priuli appear as he painfully mounts the steps onto the Quarterdeck.

Several guests go forward to help Priuli. I lurch back at the shock of seeing him and manage to steady myself by placing my hands on the balustrade, but I can't control the frenzied trembling of my knees. I grasp the shrouds to support myself. Perhaps the monk is just staring blankly before him in the effort of mounting the Quarterdeck ladder but I see a threat of vengeance in his eyes that makes the oath taken on my mother's Missal to defend the Sanmicheles no longer fanciful. I suppose that if I were one of the others nearby his glance would mean nothing, but they don't know that someone connected with the Sanmicheles tried to murder him Sunday night.

His bandaged head stands out tortoiselike from a body clad in a blue silk cloak that Augusto has lent him. Augusto also has had a long staff cut for him from the ship's reserve of timber and he clings to this weakly. Apparently he was found unconscious in the bottom of Augusto's galley after they sailed.

Had the monk staggered on board Augusto's galley in the night, half slain? Had he been carried onto the ship unconscious, and perhaps cared for by some pious sailor who would not reveal himself for fear of association with the crime?

So Nicolo has failed to murder Priuli! But why has the tongueless Murad offered himself for flogging by me? Is this somehow connected with the fact that I am one of the Sanmichele family, the family that commissioned Priuli's death? My green doublet springs to mind. I have no means of knowing how or where this has been recovered. Does Murad think I will hold him responsible for its alienation from my person? He couldn't know I have given it to Nicolo to throw away, and Nicolo may have used it as a disguise when he overtook Murad to take upon himself the business of disposing of Priuli.

The other Galley Commanders and their officers are eloquent in their praise of Augusto for so quickly getting his galley back in condition to go to sea. Their admiration for his resilience in the face of misfortune momentarily extinguishes envy of his vast wealth, and they now admire his princely ostentation. A long table is set up on the Quarterdeck and, after the shuffle that goes on amongst quests before searing themselves chance finds me where I least wanted to be, opposite Priuli. I cannot bring myself to say anything to him about his desolate state. But in saying nothing I am conscious that I am behaving guiltily, although in no way guilty. I pray that he will interpret my silence as that of an inarticulate, heedless idiot.

The younger Loredan has come over from one of the galleys and shouts down the table to greet me. He feels free here to exercise his sarcasm amongst mainly young galley officers.

"Eh! Valente, the Classical Scholar! What were you telling us about Istria at Senator Sanmichele's house? About Greeks coming and getting gold out of the water somewhere in this part. Some old Roman said the Danube once came out round about where we are going. In Istria, wasn't it?"

Most of those present take no notice of this inane remark. My reply freezes in my throat as I see that Priuli is all attention. The 'old Roman' was the geographer Strabo who is on the Inquisitor's forbidden list. Augusto Contarini-Colonna has been listening too and like a good host comes to my rescue.

"If you mean the historian, Strabo, yes, he did say something of the sort, that Jason really sailed up the Adriatic to the mouth of the Ister, the old name for the Danube, and not up the Aegean into the Black Sea. Hence the name, 'Istria'. It was here that Jason and his crew found the natives dipping sheep's wool into the river to collect the gold. This is the story of the Golden Fleece. Possibly some geological upheaval of catastrophic proportions later caused the river to change course".

This is what Paolo Loredan wants.

"Did he also say what Valente was saying, that the Parthenon temple in Athens is crooked because the Earth's axis shifted?"

Augusto doesn't trouble to answer him, but Priuli speaks and all become silent .Let me explain what happened, Signori," says he weakly,

"Jason must have been sent to Istria by the Greeks to find an architect to build the temple this Capodistrian talked about. Why? Because the Capodistrians know all about cutting up stone and marble. They found one and took him back to Athens, telling him to get to work aligning the building on the east-west line. The Capodistrians work slowly and this one would probably have taken his eastern bearing of the sun one morning when the thought occurred to him, and his western bearing some months later when his mind started working again, the sun having undergone its seasonal shift, with the result that so mystified your Strabo."

There follows a roar of hilarious acclamation as the galley officers lift their wine goblets in mock tribute to Priuli who nevertheless continues to glare at me.

Augusto Contarini-Colonna proves a good friend;

"We have some work to do, Marco. Let's send for your quadrant, and then when we've finished our food we'll go up into the bows, clear of the sails, and have some practice in taking the sun's declination."

We hail our galley, Leona, to send my quadrant across and soon see a boat being lowered. Then we turn our attention to the food set in front of us.

One of Leona's boats is coming alongside. I leap up startled when I see the head that appears above the ship's bulwarks. It is Murad rather than Osvaldo whose job it is who brings the quadrant.

Murad first looks at me and then he catches sight of Priuli sitting opposite me. He flings the quadrant onto the galley's deck and disappears quickly down into the boat. Soon we see him rowing at a ludicrous speed back to the 'Leona', his massive arms flailing the oars with more than human strength. I go to pick up my quadrant, deafened by the laughter of all present including Augusto's men and the guffaw of the sly Paolo Loredan at the spectacle Murad's desperate flight presents.

But Priuli is not laughing. He is staring blankly at the swiftly receding boat bearing a man who is evidently my servant and, from what I now know, also a hireling in some mysterious way of the Sanmicheles – a valid link in the chain connecting his plight with me! But if he has seen his attacker's face he must know it was Nicolò. And if Nicolò, perfidiously to disguise himself as me wore that green doublet it would have counted for nothing since Priuli has never seen me in that doublet. But given that the Senator father by substituting Nicolò for Murad at the last moment has spawned two potential murderers in Priuli's path Priuli may have had a chance to identify Murad and may not have seen the face of Nicolò who committed the atrocity. Manifestly there is no way I can convey that, in spite of appearances, I played not even a dormant part in the outrage he suffered.

We are now close to Fasana where we can anchor for the night so the sails are lowered and the rowers put to work. Two thirds of the men are allowed ashore until dawn. Fasana is popular with the

Venetian Navy since food and wine are exceptionally cheap here, and the girls, accustomed to ship visits, are obliging to the point of being unavoidable. So to the misery of those who have to remain on board, including the shackled Hassan, is added occasional giggles from the shoreside bushes and male grunts of satisfaction.

Augusto has ordered all the officers to remain on board the galleys since there is no suitable accommodation for them on shore and to make sure they don't have the chance to misbehave, I suppose. Osvaldo has prepared my bunk and I turn in early since Augusto's hospitality has made me sleepy. Indeed it must be the strength of his wine that is giving me such a restless night and a dream that causes me considerable embarrassment since I awake screaming in the early hours of the morning. This dream emerges, as remembered dreams always seem to come, out of an entanglement of which I can recall nothing earlier than the point where I find myself in the open space before the Church of Santa Maria Formosa in Venice, near the Sanmicheles' house, accompanied by the monk, Priuli, whose staff seems to elongate, an oddly pleasurable feeling to me, until it reaches the narrow gothic door of the church. I am slashing wildly at it with an axe, cutting it into logs that pile around me and begin to glow with a hellish crimson. Flames leap from them and the smoky tongues seem interlaced with horror. I struggle to get out of the fire but in the way of dreams my limbs won't obey and fierce pain sears my legs. I scream for help and, still screaming, struggle awake out of the nightmare to find Gravisi bending over me with mild concern, and the fiery logs become the hot covers I am kicking away from my bunk.

CHAPTER THIRTEEN

Domenico del Tacco's impatience to get a vast quantity of work done in the hours before finally sailing from Venice - work that we thought would take weeks - does little to take my mind off the fate that now must threaten Michaela. And the rest of the Sanmichele family of course. There are still many items of stores to obtain, perhaps unobtainable but at least requested, before leaving. We still have to stow the main supply of powder and ammunition. It was while I was supervising stowage of this below deck that I heard del Tacco shouting at someone angrily.

"Who told you to load those kegs onto my ship? Get them all back into your boat!"

Perhaps I have not learned much in Leona, but there is one thing I have learned well, which is that if there is trouble on board the ship it is more than likely that I am involved in some way, and I undeniably am this time. When I leap up a ladder to look I see Osvaldo standing in a boat alongside and handing up kegs to some men on deck. Seeing me, Osvaldo addresses me instead of instantly obeying del Tacco's order;

"It's from the agent Didier, Signorino Marco. Istrian wine from your own vineyards."

I know of no one likely to ship wine to Didier for me - certainly not my father. Didier must have some motive for this ingratiating step.

"Take it away," orders del Tacco. "I have barely enough stowage space for essential supplies. Certainly none for private wine cellars."

I nod to Osvaldo and he, sullenly re-embarking the kegs that he has managed to get on board the galley, starts back to Didier's store with his cargo.

"Find another servant and send that one back to Capo d'Istria," orders del Tacco. "Far from keeping him out of sight you seem to have let him take over the ship."

With del Tacco looking on I call to Osvaldo, make him come back, and give him some money and a verbal message for Didier telling that agent to look after him and return him to Capodistria when he could find the means. I also order him to tell Didier that I shall be asking for his help in finding another servant. I wish Osvaldo a safe return to Capodistria. He weeps and sets off to return the cargo of wine, no doubt pleased with the message that secures his freedom from the galley he hated so much.

In the afternoon del Tacco orders me to have wedges cut and firmly fitted under the cannon to give it the extra elevation required to get a more useful shot trajectory, a better range. Exposed for so long up on the foredeck I feel very uncomfortable and glance fearfully over my shoulder at every leather-jerkined official that passes by in a boat or on shore, fearing arrest. It is thus that I see my Veronese friend passing along the jetty and on an impulse yell at him to wait for me. I finish what I am doing and make my way ashore quickly.

"What happened to you on Sunday?" he asks.

"I thought you had already left."

"You must think I'm even more of a cockerel than you are! The Madame told me that YOU were in and out of there in less than five minutes."

"Never mind that now. I have to meet someone in secret. Can you help me?"

He backs away holding up the palm of his hand.

"The last words my father said to me were not to have confidences with Capodistrians. Is it a girl?"

"Yes, it is my cousin." Then I am aghast at myself, having said so much so soon.

"But Venice is equipped for such assignations. Haven't you noticed the covered gondolas? Do you know a time when she is likely to be away from home, and where she is likely to go?"

"There is only one answer that I know - most evenings she will probably be at Benediction at the Church of Santa Maria Formosa, accompanied by her slave girl."

A new interest shines in the Veronese's eyes at the mention of the slave girl.

"Let's go," he says. "It is near the hour of Benediction."

We walk to a point within easy distance of the church and I stand aside as he makes arrangements with a gondolier. Now I am heartily sorry that I have involved him in this trysting. I should have thought of this contrivance myself. I step down into the cabin, luxuriously carpeted and velvet curtained. And we glide away to the canal steps leading to the square before the church of Santa Maria Formosa. He stands up on deck with the gondolier. We wait for the girls to come out through the great gothic doors. My impatience will not let me wait in the gondola and I mount the canal steps. I regret my impetuosity since this is the hour when many upstanding Venetian patricians attend Confession, and I am afraid to bring suspicion on my love simply by being seen with her. As she comes out of church she looks very downcast but accepts my presence almost as though she expects me, and we climb down into the gondola.

"You must escape, Michaela." I take her hands in mine.

"Yes. I must escape."

The gondolier, egged on by the Veronese, is singing a shameless love song. I wish that I ordered a second gondola for the Veronese and the slave girl, who now is with him on deck. The Veronese are not in the least discriminating I realize.

"Signorino, Alloh!" comes a shout from the slave girl, then she thrusts her head down through the curtains to explain, and "It's the Signorino Nicolò, Signorina. He is on the bridge with his big sword on."

This is the requital I expect. The brother is there to vindicate the honour of his sister, a sister about to take the veil! There can be no planning her escape. I put my head up through the curtains to order the gondolier to the side so that I might leap out and run for safety.

"Where are you going, Marco?"

"I was hoping to save you, but here I shall get myself killed instead - either by your brother or your father."

"It is my father who is in danger of death!" She looks puzzled. "And he wants to see you because you can help him, if you will." She tells gondolier to go to the Sanmichele house. "We cannot talk here!"

"I hired the gondola precisely so that we could talk privately. Can it be safe to come into your house after........?"

She gives a bitter little laugh and draws back the curtains to direct the confused gondolier, turning to me to say;

"Safe? Where is safe with Priuli alive," obviously knowing that they have tried to murder him.

I pay the gondolier enough to cover his hire for the rest of the evening, leave the Veronese and the Circassian girl in it, and fearfully follow Michaela up through the house into the salone. As we enter, the Senator springs up from a chair to confront me, Nicolò at his side. I go down on one knee saying;

"I plead for the hand of Michaela in marriage, Signor Senatore, hoping to stave off his fury.

Even as I look up at him I see that Marcantonio Sanmichele is a sadly changed man. The glow of power has faded from him, and he seems to have shrunk. There is greyness about him that I have not noticed before.

"Come with me."

The Senator leads me out onto the balcony. It crosses my mind that he must be intending to throw me into the canal below. Michaela and Nicolò remain quietly in the room. Once out on the balcony I notice that a heavy black cloud hangs over the city to the east, in foreboding contrast to the sunset gold reflected in the water under the canal bridge to our right.

"Marco," he says, putting his arm around my shoulder, "Marco, You haven't time for marriage in Venice. But my little Michaela has a wild plan which will save her from being used by Priuli in the way Nicolò has explained to you."

I recall that he himself had made an odd remark about Michaela taking the veil. That was on the day we arrived when we were being received by the Doge; and I have pondered over it a great deal.

"If you will excuse me, Ser Sanmichele, I was under the impression that only the father could give permission or refuse permission to have his daughter taken into a convent."

"How can I refuse permission?"

He is talking to himself rather than to me, yet in a way I know that his words are carefully chosen for their effect on me.

"Priuli came this morning. He repeated his demand for Michaela, and whether she stays here or goes to stay with her mother they will find her, and where else can she go?" He squeezed my shoulders, then stood back and placed his two hands on my head as a priest blesses one.

"And you?" I ask uncomfortably, "Aren't you in danger, Ser Sanmichele?"

"Oh, Yes! But the process of destroying me will take some time. I am a Senator, and there are formalities. Meanwhile we have thought of a way of getting Michaela out and to Corfu, where my wife's brother is Prefect. The Provveditore told you what orders were being issued to the Capodistrian galley. Corfu is one of the places where you will call before joining the Allied Fleets. I am happy to give you Michaela in marriage. The wedding can be arranged in Corfu by the Prefect, and Michaela will of course remain under his care until your mission is over. You will carry my letter to him. May the Blessing of the Lord be upon you, my son, when you sail from Venice? Whatever you and Michaela do be sure that she has her father's blessing and, in event of trouble, you will have my support as long as I have any power."

He takes his hands from my head and guides me back into the salone, and then indicates to Nicolò that they all should leave Michaela and me to ourselves. Thus the father whose anger I was dreading hands over to me for my private delectation the girl for whom I was burning with desire - and with his blessing!

"It will give us time to find a solution to our own problems, Marco," advises Nicolò almost apologetically, giving me a cousinly kiss as he follows his father out.

I don't know whether Nicolò's reasoning was pronounced in good faith or not, and whether he is serious. I am so overjoyed that this awful male barrier has been overcome that it doesn't enter my head to suspect Sanmichele's motives, although had I been better schooled in the ways of the world I would have known well that such a break with convention must spring from some powerful economic incentive.

There was a powerful incentive: a rich marriage for the Sanmichele daughter. This did not at the time occur to me, perhaps because I had always been accustomed to my father's resources. And it was only later when we were at sea, with Michaela disguised as my male servant, that I realized that an important consideration could be that in Venetian eyes she would now be compromised for all time by coming alone with me, unmarried. That is, if I didn't marry her at the first opportunity, which is all I wanted to do in any case, and which Priuli was threatening to make impossible. Even if she escaped the convent he could see to it that no priest would be given permission to marry me to my first cousin in ordinary circumstances.

"What happened to Cesare?" was all I could think of to say to Michaela.

"My father finally threw him out, after his misbehaviour."

"What? He misbehaved again?" I demand thinking of what Nicolò had thrashed him for.

"I mean when he laughed at us.......When......"

"You mean that your father knows?"

"He was in his library. Certainly he heard Cesare." Then she came close and put her head against my chest. "Marco, don't be angry with me. I have everything ready to leave with you for Corfu when the galley sails. My father says it's a short voyage, and will only be taking me from my father's protection into the protection of my uncle, the Prefect of Corfu. But although my father is the head of the Navy it's better not to draw attention to myself, and he doesn't want to entangle the Capodistrian Galley Commander, so I will look exactly like a male servant. No one will ever know." (Evidently they were even informed of my need for someone to replace Osvaldo, and had calculated that Michaela, well disguised as a boy, could be taken for that someone - but such detailed scheming wouldn't have occurred to me.

She kept her head low, waiting for my answer. Although I set out to save the maiden, I have no plan of my own, and I am by now utterly bewildered by the Sanmichele family. I cannot resist her, so I deliberately choose not to think what such an outrageous scheme entails.

CHAPTER FOURTEEN

The masts of the Allied Fleets transform the Sicilian harbor of Messina into a leafless forest. More than two hundred galleys, six galleasses and a dozen fleet support ships lie there, grouped in nations.

Messina city has become a pleasure park for eighty thousand soldiers and sailors who flood the flag-bedecked streets by night and by day in search of pleasure. Supplies of local Sicilian wines run out and imported Italian wine flows from the fountains in the city squares. Those tired of Arabian girls are entertained by couplings between gigantic Maltese women and blue, serious faced, Sicilian donkeys

These exhibitions are decorously suspended when processions bearing images of saints, borne on the shoulders of incense-swinging acolytes, move through the crowd to remind Spaniards, Tuscans, Savoians, Milanese, Romans, Mantuans, Venetians and all that form the Holy League, of their common mortality.

The gallows at the harbor entrance is also a reminder of mortality. Equal numbers of Spanish and Italian bodies swing there, condemned to die by Marcantonio Colonna who commands the Papal galleys as a warning against continual street fights between these races. Venetian bodies are among those hanging from the long horizontal pole.

In performing my duty as Flag Lieutenant to the Venetian Admiral, I carefully avoid all such distractions on the afternoon of Saturday, 15 September. When I leave the Citadel where the Commander-in-Chief, Don John of Austria, has his headquarters, to make for the eastern end of the harbor where the Venetian Fleet lies, I skirt the city centre so as to travel faster on my borrowed mount. I am conveying to Veniero his copy of Don John's sailing orders and I already know enough of Admiral Veniero not to expect any further pleasure from life if I lose these in some fray. Veniero has waited too long has fought too long for this positive sign that the Fleets really are to sail and fight the Muslims. He is now impatient to assemble and address the Venetians before the galleys put to sea.

But the unexpectedness of Don John of Austria's orders to sail oblige me to perform one very necessary deviation from my route between the Citadel and the Flagship of Venice. This is to collect Michaela from a desolate cottage outside the city where she is now accommodated. The elderly signora, the only occupant, is happy to accept my gold in return for looking after Michaela, promising to tell no one, especially not the parish priest.

We, that is Michaela and I, have no plans for the future. Circumstances dictate our present situation and another circumstance now dictates that I get her on board the only place of refuge I knew, the Flagship of Venice, before we leave Messina. What makes this imperative, in my censurable mind, is the discovery in that same visit to the Citadel that Ludovico Priuli is amongst the Holy Men, Dominicans and Franciscans, who have been ordered by the Pope to wait in attendance upon Don John of Austria. I, of course, egoistically, conclude that Priuli has engineered a place for himself at the Messina headquarters suspecting Michaela might be near, and intending to cause trouble for the Sanmicheles and me by exposing our iniquity to the world.

But to revert for a moment to when we left Venice: Michaela was brought on board our galley by Murad immediately before finally sailing (this was an arrangement that I expected, now aware of how much Murad was in the confidence of the Sanmicheles).

She looked, she and I thought, very much like a boy servant would be expected to look. They planned her arrival for a time when Domenico del Tacco's attention would be occupied in ensuring that his ship left harbor in good order, anxious as he would be to show that the Capodistrian galley was as smart as the Venetian galleys we sailed with.

But he remained deceived by us for a very short time, if at all. He called me to his quarters when the ship was clear of the harbor and had settled down to a north-westerly breeze.

"I am not going to allow you to make this Capodistrian galley look foolish in the eyes of the Venetians. In days, with a lucky wind, we shall be at Messina............."

"Messina?"

"Yes, Messina."

"I understood that the orders issued by the Signoria said that we would call at Corfu before arriving at Messina."

"There was no reason for you to understand anything. I am in command of this ship, and I am not a slave of the Signoria. If I find the wind is favourable I shall round Santa Maria di Leuca and make straight for Messina where the Allied Fleets are to assemble rather than give the rowers unnecessary labour in taking the ship to Corfu."

"But I am to be married to Senator Sanmichele's daughter at Corfu!"

The words were out before I could reflect on them. Perhaps in that instant I thought to impress him by mentioning the man who was head of the Venetian Navy. It was of no avail. Frostily he said;

"I did not hear that remark, and don't repeat it. There are limits to what is permitted in this Capodistrian galley. It is better for me not to know that they have been exceeded since I might be forced to take disciplinary action that would be regrettable for you, me, and Capo d'Istria. As you know, your orders are to leave my ship at Messina for Admiral Veniero's Flagship. What you do after is not my concern. Meanwhile what I said about Osvaldo being kept out of sight applies even more to your new servant. You will half clear out that small store next to Gravisi's cabin personally, now. The gear you clear out you will stow in your own cabin. You will fit a bunk into the space in the store left by what you clear out and your new servant will remain in this. You will be responsible for supplying your servant with anything required but naturally you will not enter that store, and you both will leave my ship as soon as the ship arrives at Messina. I shall try to get rid of Murad, too."

Speechless, I leave his quarters to set about carrying out his orders. Perhaps he knew about us even before we sailed and had decided that it would not help him to raise an issue involving the flight of the daughter of the Senator responsible for the Navy. But this was to suppose that he also knew that Sanmichele connived in her escape, otherwise he would have thought it his duty to bring the affair to official attention. If he knew who was his informant? He would have told Gravisi and di Giovanni who most likely regarded my action as typical of already depraved modern nobility.

For me to have Michaela so close under these conditions was an unexpected torture. Murad brought her to the Aftercastle from under the compartment below the rambade deck where she timidly waited. Now Murad is waiting for me, seeming to know already that I will require his help in making these wretched arrangements for her.

The passage from Venice to Messina in the 'Leona' passed very uncomfortably, both from a physical and a social point of view. Now at last I was able to take Michaela ashore at Messina and find for her the accommodation I have mentioned.

We dismount behind some harbor buildings, out of sight of the galleys, and she waits for me whilst I arrange to have the borrowed horse returned, and then follows me (as my servant) on board the Flagship.

The Venetian Flagship is spacious compared with the Capodistrian galley, and for the moment at least, I am satisfied that no one on board suspects that my servant is a girl except Murad who knows. For him a place has easily been found in the crew of the undermanned Flagship. Murad cannot tell anyone even if he wishes and I feel confident enough to get him to prepare a sleeping place for Michaela below the suspended bunk in the cabin allocated to me. Then I lose no time in reporting to Admiral Veniero in his quarters with Don John's sailing orders.

When the Admiral had read the orders he sent for his Galley Commander;

"Tell the officers of all the Venetian galleys to assemble on the jetty under the stern of this ship. I will address them from the stern balustrade."

"Signorsi!"

"I want only Venetian officers. That is, I do not want the army officers in the pay of Spain to be present: those who have been placed on board my galleys without my permission."

When it is reported to him that all Venetian officers are assembled he goes up onto his Quarterdeck and, in the silence following the trumpet call heralding his appearance by the huge triple lantern, he stands erect in figure, powerful of voice, and with little save his white hair and white beard to indicate his seventy-five years and he points upwards to the main peak of the Flagship where the Lion Banner of Venice lifts to the breeze.

"What is the meaning of the Latin words written on the pages of the book which the Lion holds under his paw?" he demands.

"Peace to Thee, my Apostle," comes the reply from many voices.

"Peace!" exclaims Veniero, "Peace, my fellow Venetians, is for the strong. Peace comes from strength. I will quote another Latin phrase, 'QUI DESIDERAT PACEM PRAEPARET BELLUM' which first appeared a military manual written by Flavius Vegetus Renatus in the fourth century of Our Lord."

Turning to a robed figure at his shoulder, the Chaplain General of the Venetian Fleet, for whom Veniero had found space in a galley other than his own Flagship, he orders loudly;

"Tell them what it means."

"He who wishes for peace must prepare for war," says the Chaplain.

"Louder! They can't hear you," commands the Admiral.

"HE WHO WISHES FOR PEACE MUST PREPARE FOR WAR," booms the Chaplain.

Veniero continuous:

"When the Republic seems secure the brays of Asses reverberate loud through the council chambers of Venice. Falsely reassured the Republic devotes to other purposes the money that should go to construct new warships and to keep the old ones in good condition. It allows young nobles to degenerate into wastrels or money-makers, leaving the Navy without officers. Left without money to pay volunteers properly we find convicts and fugitives from justice chained to the rowing benches.........."

At these words I recall a painful image: I remember overtaking Gravisi on the jetty on first going ashore early that morning, and he called me back to tell me about Hassan. They found a chain draped untidily over the gunwales of the Leona. Men were ordered to haul it inboard. The end was shackled to Hassan's ankles, and as they lifted him into the ship they saw that his hands were hooked in death, retaining the form they had taken as he clung to an underwater hull projection to prevent himself from being hauled up so as to be sure to drown. They found a marlinspike which he used to force away sufficient chain, still lying under the thwart. I try to shake off the cruel image and force my attention back to what the Admiral was saying.

"Between political dreams and reality has always lain this barrier; the inability to learn that there is a price to pay for maritime unpreparedness and always in the end we pay it with the blood of valiant men."

"Now, with fire and sword, the Muslims are overrunning land and sea, almost to the threshold of Venice herself; laying waste Crete, taking Zante, Cerigo and Cephalonia, sacking Dulcigno, Antivari, Curzola and Lesina, burning Budua and many fortresses. Does it surprise you that as we lie in harbor day after day my mind is flooded with ever mounting shame at weeks so uselessly spent in trying to convince the Spaniards that we must fight?"

"It was no plan of mine to come to Messina. My intention was to anticipate the Ottoman advance and relieve Cyprus. But, obeying the Senate's command, I gave credit to their reasoning that, as a focal point of all routes to the Eastern Mediterranean this port of Messina could be the springboard from which an assault on the main Ottoman Fleet by the combined Christian Fleets could be launched."

"Launched? Instead we have launched countless conferences to listen to countless reasons as to why we should not fight. That faithless temporiser and mastermind of intrigue, Gianandrea Doria of Genova, qualified as the champion debater."

"This Holy League, this Alliance, was called together by His Holiness the Pope to help the Venetians hold back the Muslim from Christendom. Yet over weeks I have had to listen to plans for dissipating the combined fleets in side issues such as the re-taking of Tunis leaving the main enemy Fleet untouched. Since it is already far into the year such diversions would leave little time for naval warfare, and would allow the Muslims another winter in which to redouble the strength of their already formidable fleet."

"Our duty is clear, my friends. Although the year is far advanced, we are at last to sail and search out and destroy the Ottoman Fleet. We have suffered many humiliations; the Senate let our fleet degenerate to a point where we could not face the enemy without the help of other nations. We have suffered the indignity of taking on board our ships the soldiers of other nations since we are deficient there too. Furthermore these soldiers are to be commanded by non-Venetian officers who whilst serving on board the Republic's ships will owe their allegiance to Philip of Spain."

"I, your Admiral, and faithful servant of Venice over years that are for you lost in history, ask you NOT to forget these slights. At last we are moving out to find the enemy. Let these and all the other humiliations that Venice has suffered and will suffer in the days to come kindle deep in your souls a burning obsession to avenge her, so that the outcome of the battle will leave her with unsullied glory, and our accompanying 'allies' with incontrovertible proof that Victory would still have come to Venice had THEY remained at home."

Veniero lifts his hand to still the loud cries of assent, holding up a sheaf of documents;

"These are the orders I have just received. My friend here, Agostino Barbarigo, will command the Venetian left wing of the combined fleets which will consist of fifty-three galleys. The centre will consist of sixty-four galleys and will come directly under the Commander-in-Chief, Don John of Austria, and I will be close to his ship in this, my Flagship of Venice. The right wing consisting of fifty-four galleys will be commanded by del Cardona. Fortunately for us, Gianandrea Doria of Genova has been placed on the far side of the right wing. His presence in any part of the Fleet can only assist the enemy."

"The squadrons will be distinguished by coloured pendants worn at the main peak - blue for the centre, yellow for the left wing, and green for the right wing. The rearguard consisting of thirty-five galleys will be distinguished by white pendants and will be commanded by the Marquis of Santa Cruz, who will observe the progress of the battle and give assistance where required. The Venetian galleasses will be divided between the three squadrons, and instructions as to their deployment will follow. In order to make identification between Christian and Muslim clear in the heat of battle large Venetian ensigns are to be flown from tall staffs set against the Quarterdeck balustrades of your galleys, whatever other identification is carried in the rigging."

"I would only add that the fleets have been deployed in this manner on my insistence that they must be closely knit to avoid repetition of the disaster that befell the old Andrea Doria of Genova at Prevesa when his endless straggling line of ships were picked off one by one by Barbarossa who is said to have laughed to the end of his days at the manner in which Doria fled. Doria having prematurely lit his stern lantern extinguished it in the hope of remaining unseen although silhouetted against the brilliant western evening sky. But enough of this....”

“Many Venetian ships were lost on that occasion, but one lesson learnt must not be forgotten and that is the damage done by the fire power of the Great Galleon of Venice.”

“With this in mind, I have recommended that the Venetian galleasses be so placed as to allow them to use their powerful artillery to break up the enemy at the outset of battle. But my orders are that the artillery mounted in the galleys is not to be wasted at ineffective range. The crash of your ship’s beak in the enemy’s side and the roar of your guns should be heard at the same time.”

“And if, as Venetian officers, you are so privileged as to give orders to Spanish-paid militia on board your own ships, tell them not to fire their arquebuses until they are close enough to be splashed by the blood of the enemy.”

“But remember, above all, that if our common love for Venice is translated into valour and ardent loyalty to one another we cannot fail to rend the veil of terror that too long has hung over the Mediterranean and threatens all Europe.

CHAPTER FIFTEEN

The night is spent in clearing the sailors and soldiers out of the bars and brothels and ensuring that they are returned to their ships. Taking petty officers with us we scour all the likely places and by the early hours Messina is clear except no doubt for some who are successfully hidden.

At dawn the ships begin to move out of the harbor. By mid-morning all the Fleet is assembled, spread wide across the straits of Messina. All await the exit of Don John of Austria. At midday the roar of Messina's saluting guns signal the exit from the harbor of the enormous, three-lantern, heavily embellished and gaily be flagged Royal Galley of Spain.

From the decks of the far-stretched line of galleys we, in shining armour, hail our boy Commander-in-Chief - Don John - as he takes up station at the head of the Allied Fleets. Timed by the drums oars rise and fall in tens of thousands as the galleys fan out across the sun-flooded blue plain of the Central Mediterranean. Banners, streamers, and the standards of the nobility of Europe lift lightly to the breeze created by the advance of the ships containing Europe's last hope against the Muslim hordes

This waking dream of glory fed by the pageant unfolding before my eyes and by the fresh memory of Veniero's plea for loyalty fired again the boyish idealism that has driven me to the galleys. Memories of the Venice of religious and financial intrigue became indistinct and unreal. I can be fairly precise about the moment when guilt with its various cutting edges began to sear my mind. The trumpet call telling the officers to fall out, to go below deck, and change from armour into normal dress sounds. As I turn to leave the Quarterdeck and go below I become guiltily aware that I am, disloyally to Michaela, thinking of her presence on board as more than simply an embarrassment. For the first time I see it clearly as an unpardonable betrayal of moral rectitude which Veniero would consider profoundly disloyal to him and be the last to condone. Exposure will mean disgrace and I will become a figure of derision and contempt before thousands. Another cutting edge of guilt is the re-awakened consciousness of disloyalty to my father who has warned me not to get involved in Venetian wiles. He probably had his brother-in-law, Marcantonio Sanmichele, in mind when he gave this advice.

Murad is in my cabin with Michaela when I enter. Indeed, I wondered how he could be absent so much from the rowing benches without getting into trouble with his officers, although I am glad to see him there to help me out of my armour. Then I dismiss him.

We see what we want to see, and I want to see Michaela well disguised as a boy servant, if not a manservant. I now see her in a new light, and realise that until that moment I deceived myself. Tight fitting pale blue hose and a short black belted grey tunic reveal too well her sex. Fair strands of silken hair that refuse to be bunched up under her bulky floppy hat softened her already most unmasculine facial contours.

"Murad? Has he been troubling you?"

"No! Why should he trouble me?" She is surprised at the question.

And what if he had troubled her? I could hardly have a dumb rower flogged for troubling my 'male' attendant: well, in a Spanish galley perhaps, but not in a Venetian one.

"He is helping, Marco! You and I acted in panic at Messina. Priuli would never have found me. He will go back to Venice now that the ships have left Messina. You could have given me enough money to let me stay there for months. In time you could have got a message back to Venice in a dispatch vessel and Didier or some agent would eventually have looked after me. Now it is clear that we must go to Ser Veniero and explain everything. Obviously he knows my father well and through him is responsible to the Senate and Doge. What reason has he not to understand and help?"

I am aghast at the prospect of facing Veniero and wonder how far I would get with the explanation before being manacled and locked up below under guard until I could be thrown into prison in some convenient fortress along the coast. She studies my face and says;

"You must have the courage to do this Marco otherwise when he discovers us it will be worse for you and for my family."

Perhaps she is hinting at the oath Nicolò had extracted from me, or could it be that she is just more clear-headed and practical? I cannot find words to reply, but after a long embrace I explain that I had better go for dinner with the others, where I was expected, after which we could talk about it again.

When I arrive in the officers' dining quarters that occupy the aftermost part of the ship on the deck immediately below the Quarterdeck and are therefore illuminated by the great insloping windows set in the galley's stern, I find assembled there Loredans, Contarinis, Bragadins, and the rest of the Venetian nobility. Pasquale Loredan, Veniero's Chief of Staff, who stood alongside the Admiral at the conferences of the past weeks, now feels free, since Veniero has retired to his own quarters, to expand on the difficulties Venetians have with the Allies;

"That we are finally out at sea together is a miracle. Yesterday morning I would not have believed it possible. After days of discussion leading up to an agreement to sail together to find the enemy fleet Gianandrea Doria finally reached Messina with his eleven galleys and almost reversed all our decisions."

"After all those weeks of argument!" comments Gaspero Contarini, Veniero's Chief Navigator. "It seems to me that Don John's views are being continually adjusted to coincide with those of the last man that gets his hearing."

"He is young," says Pasquale Loredan. "Anyway the newly arrived Gianandrea Doria states all those reasons for not fighting which have been reiterated so often. Reasons that have been so often fought and defeated by Veniero, as though he, Doria, was the first to think of them: that the Ottoman Fleet is twice the size of ours, that we lack sufficient militia, that it is too late in the year, that victory will only mean that the enemy will spend the winter building a bigger fleet, that coming out of port we shall be at a disadvantage in facing a fleet waiting for us at sea, that we should not risk this great fleet we have assembled in fighting the Ottoman Fleet but should go for Tunis and the Muslim pirates."

"That would drive Veniero almost mad," says someone just entered. He looks around and asks in wonderment whether there were some present who could return to their homes and admit that they had never met the enemy face to face."

I think myself that Veniero will certainly fear to return to Venice and submit those reasons for not engaging the Ottoman Fleet, knowing the fate of his failed predecessor, Admiral Zane who was executed for failing to do just that.

"The Admiral would find it difficult to suppress his anger at such words," continues Pasquale Loredan, who by the way is the uncle of the detestable Paolo Loredan, whose presence somewhere in that fleet contributes to increase my sense of guilt and fear of general exposure. "He's had to suppress his anger even to the point of accepting an intermingling of Spanish galleys in the order of battle in case we Venetians decide not to obey Don John's deployment orders. That, or with the more insulting implication that we may fly from the enemy unless watched over by the Spaniards."

The outburst of rage from the dozen or so assembled officers changes to hilarity and my heart skips a beat as he starts talking about Priuli;

"And to see that we say our prayers His Holiness the Pope has seen fit to appoint that monk, Priuli, to liaise between Don John and Veniero. But Priuli, so I understand, is too comfortable in the Royal Galley of Spain to come and lie rough on board this ship."

Our Nemesis was so close, then! What chance exists that Michaela and I can continue to deceive so many especially now that monster is so near physically and administratively? I pray that he will be amongst the dead in the battle that I expect to come soon. I carefully stay on at the table until most have eaten and are leaving, now afraid that my hurried departure might be linked with mention of Priuli, and arouse suspicion.

There are other insults from the Spaniards, so they relate. In the night, while I was helping to clear the town, Spanish guard boats moved through the Venetian galleys drawing attention with loud trumpet calls to trivial orders promulgated by Don John's staff officers without prior reference to any Venetian authority.

"Blood will be shed among the Allies ere Muslim blood is shed," comments pessimistically a Bragadin or Contarini. "We shall have to anchor this Fleet once or twice again in the shelter of some bay or other before we find the enemy, and fighting will break out between us. I hope I am mistaken."

I go back to the cabin and Michaela, now decided in my own mind that I must face up to the wrath of Veniero. I must go alone to him and confess that I had the Senator Sanmichele's daughter on board, and hope that he mercifully will find a quiet solution that will allow me to continue my service and avoid disgrace in the eyes of all.

"Mio Dio! It is impossible now," declares Michaela when I told her of Priuli's appointment to liaise with Veniero and that consequently I now think it better to follow her suggestion and go to Veniero. "How ever can I leave this ship before Priuli comes on board to perform his duty and talk with Veniero? If Veniero knows about us how can he fail to tell the representative of the Holy Office of such a mortal sin as we have committed, and he will ask for Priuli's counsel. Priuli will advise isolating me until I can be safely put behind convent walls, and to reinforce his arguments do you think that he will not tell Veniero that my father has accepted money from the French? And do you think that you or I will receive any mercy from Veniero when he hears that? My father will be shamed and when the report goes back to Venice the allegation will be investigated and he will be tried and ... and...."

She couldn't get the words out, but was more successful in my case:

"And YOUR name will be infamous throughout the Venetian Navy!"

CHAPTER SIXTEEN

The Flagship of Venice moves abreast the Royal Galley of Spain at about two cables distant on her port side and equidistant on the starboard side of the Royal Galley is Marcantonio Colonna's galley, the Papal Flagship.

With deteriorating weather on the second day the wind comes close on the port bow and is of little use to the lateens that remain furled. The labouring rowers make poor headway against seas that are whipped up to savage crests as we creep under the toe of Italy.

Veniero tells me that one of my duties is to take a boat and go on board the Royal Galley each day to collect any dispatches intended for the Venetians, in this way to circumvent Spanish visits to us, since he abhorred Spanish feet on his decks. The Royal Galley - Don John's Flagship - is where Priuli is doing his liaison duties. Fate seems determined to place me under Priuli's nose. I take care to keep this new risk secret from Michaela who fortunately is incurious as to my duties. Moreover I am sorry to hear that this mission is to be carried out at noon. At this hour I would prefer to be working on a table of noon declinations relating them with as much accuracy as I could to known shore bearings and dead reckoning.

But one does not question Veniero's orders. Well before noon on Monday a boat is lowered into the waves and some of the most powerful men in the ship are detailed to pull me over to the side of the Royal Galley. Ordering the men to place the boat as close to the rising and falling stern of the galley as possible I select the right moment and fling myself at the hand grips on the Royal Galley's side abaft the oar banks. With difficulty I claw my way up the hull and clamber on board while my boat plunges wildly in the turbulent seas, waiting for me.

The Royal Galley of Spain is by far the largest of the ships. Overwhelmed by her unrivalled splendour I mount the gilded steps that lead to her Quarterdeck assuming that it is to someone there that

I am intended to report my mission. Against the balustrade stands Don John of Austria, lithe and handsome, his dark steel breastplate inlaid with gold, and with a high white ruff, mantlet, and azure-plumed gilded helmet. He is holding good-humoured banter with some of his staff officers. Without acknowledging my polite bow they glance coldly in my direction, Don John caressing his long fair moustaches. I am quickly directed by a sentry back down the steps I have just come up as though my feet are profaning sacred ground and told to find de Soto, Don John's secretary. On inquiry I find him in a large compartment below in the After Castle in a compartment lined with delicate cabinetwork and illuminated by the galley's stern windows. He to ignores me and after standing there for some time, dreading the appearance of the Dominican, I am asked what I want by a junior secretary and given the dispatches I have come for.

On return to the Flagship Veniero stands waiting for me on deck, his grey cloak flapping in the rising wind. He takes the dispatches out of my hands and makes for his own quarters. If, as is most likely, he hopes for intelligence regarding proximity of the Turkish Fleet, which might have helped substantiate his advice to go and find and fight them he must be disappointed. He summons a meeting of his senior officers in the late afternoon where I am as usual obliged to attend on him. He has allowed a few hours for his re-ignited anger to cool. We are told that the dispatches contain a letter from Priuli.

"You will remember," he addresses his officers, "that in my speech to the Venetians I mentioned that Agostino Barbarigo will command the left wing of the combined fleets when we come to battle. Effectively this means that he will be in operational command of the Venetian galleys and I shall be an advisor, as the senior Venetian officer on Don John's staff, floating alongside his Royal Galley. Although for obvious reasons I have not mentioned it to the Venetians who assembled at Messina, in fact I have not been consulted as to Barbarigo's appointment, although I agree with it. I should have been consulted, but I was not. The Dominican monk, Ludovico Priuli appointed by the Holy Office to liaise with me was, however, consulted and now he has the effrontery to write to me to explain why HE advised the Spanish Staff to place Agostino Barbarigo in command of the galleys."

Sympathy with the Admiral in his humiliation is written in every sombre face. They are well aware that Barbarigo can deal with the

Spanish Allies better than Veniero. A quiet and reflective man, Barbarigo is renowned for his skill in confronting arrogance with a devastatingly quiet statement of the truth, and as a genius in seizing advantage out of adverse situations. He is known to be quite indifferent to considerations of personal glory, influenced only by his love of Venice and ever thoughtful for the well-being of Venetians who fought with him for her. But nevertheless each one of those veterans feels himself diminished by the contempt for Venetian pride implied in the omission to consult Veniero.

"I trust that Priuli never sets foot on board my ship."

Veniero's comment marks the beginning of the rift between Veniero and the monk that was never to be healed, and which I secretly and mistakenly, hail as a stroke of good fortune for Michaela and me.

There are no further noon visits to the Royal Galley; the weather has so deteriorated throughout these days as to make them impossible. The ablest suffer from seasickness when below deck and one may imagine that social intercourse is forgotten. This gives me an unlooked for respite from fear of discovery. It is a respite hard earned: Michaela hardly moves from where she lies despondent, except occasionally to kneel and pray to a small statue of the Madonna that she has brought with her. She remains unconvinced by my cheerful reassurance that the ship is not breaking up. I myself think it is sometimes down there amidst the thunder of the impacting seas and the groaning and straining of overcharged timbers.

"You must find a priest from one of the other ships who will confess me, Marco. We shall be drowned. It can't be long. I must confess before I die."

"Confess?"

"It is too late to worry about what anybody thinks now. I am in mortal sin."

"Our sins are not mortal ones, Michaela."

"Incest is a mortal sin, I am sure. Have you forgotten that we are first cousins?"

Lugubrious religious imaginings have not troubled me, although, inconsistently the horror of breaking the oath that I had taken on my mother's Missal comes often into my thoughts; but I don't believe we shall founder. I am certain that I cannot find a priest to brave the seas and come across to our priestless Flagship, and it appals me to reflect that Michaela's guileless religiosity now risks betraying her into the very trap that has been set to snare her father, the avoidance of which is the reason for her presence with me in that ship in the first place.

Work required on deck is the excuse I give her for postponing this holy mission and I make myself useful to the Galley Commander, acting as a go-between with the unruly Spanish soldiery. Admittedly this also serves as an excuse for not always being by Veniero's side. Guilt makes me feel uncomfortable in his presence. Absurdly, I imagine him turning to me and asking innocently or, I dread, roguishly;

"And how was Senator Marcantonio Sanmichele when we left Venice, and his two children, Nicolò and Michaela as I remember?"

CHAPTER SEVENTEEN

The seas are snatching cruelly at the weather bank of oars and bruised rowers blaspheme at savage blows from the heavy looms. Veniero's Galley Commander orders the drummer to slow the drumbeat to half the normal rowing rate and petty officers run up and down the centre gangway urging and correcting the oar swing to the new rhythm of deeper and longer strokes. Then the weather oar banks are ordered inboard, allowing greater pulling power on the lee banks to compensate for the force of the wind on the ship's head.

My self-imposed go-between duties oblige me to intervene in infuriating incidents caused by the aimless milling around of the Spanish soldiery, when the whips of our petty officers, hardly ever used on the Venetian rowers, are raised menacingly against our uninvited passengers.

The weather is worsening. Faintly borne on the gale comes the trumpeter's call from the Royal Galley now commanding re-orientation of the fleet towards the shelter of the land, and the disarrayed squadrons turn in towards Cape Spartivento. The bows of the galleys are now up into the wind and it requires hours of agonizing rowing to bring the ships under the lee of the headland where we are to lie that night.

When the ships have found suitable anchor holding ground and are as distanced as not to foul one another in swinging at anchor, in so far as this is possible for such a large assembly, commenced the work of settling the men for the night. The additional soldiery embarked makes this no easy matter, and disputes between these and the Venetians occasionally lead to blows, something that would never have taken place amongst the well-disciplined Venetian galley crews.

The next day foul weather continues. We take the Fleet to sea in the morning but are forced back under Spartivento to wait for the wind to moderate. We put to sea again in the night. In the course of

Wednesday, 19 September, we pass Cape Stilo. But when we arrive off Cape Colonna in the evening we again meet winds of such force that further progress is impossible and once more the Allied Fleets have to run for shelter. The next day brings disaster to some ships amongst them the galley of the Knights of St John, who have been settled by the Pope in Malta after the Muslims took their headquarter island, Rhodes. Their ship is lost with no survivors.

I take care to mention nothing of this to Michaela. Instead we brood over our personal problems. Yes, she admitted, it was wrong of Nicolò to disguise himself in my cast off clothes but she insists he couldn't imagine but that he would be successful and a dead Priuli would have been a menace to no one. She said that on the night of the attempted murder Nicolò had come within sight of Murad near Contarina-Colonna's galley, which was hidden in a canal close to where the monk's boat left for the island of San Stephano, and where they knew he must pass that night. But Murad seeing a figure coming upon him in the dark had fled up an alley. So, I said, Priuli might have mistaken Nicolò for me disguised as he was in my discarded tunic. She agrees, observing that since her father had forbidden any shouting Nicolò didn't use his voice. This would explain Murad's look of terror when he saw me sitting with what should have been Priuli's corpse when he came to deliver the quadrant.

That is what I thought at one point in our discussion but, on silent reflection, could I have misinterpreted the ex-slave master's flight thinking that he was driven by terror at seeing a 'resurrected' Priuli? Perhaps it was the very prospect of my 'talking' to the Dominican that terrified him - for what I knew or might know as a Sanmichele cousin of his intended part in the Sanmichele plot that Sunday evening. I suddenly remember that in one of my conversations with Michaela I was astonished when she disclosed that Murad shared his devotion almost equally between Sanmicheles and Dominicans. She related that in years past, in Cyprus, a Dominican monk had hidden him and nursed him after his tongue had been put out by the Turks before bringing him to Venice and into the service of the Sanmichele family. It occurred to me that perhaps Murad had accepted the mission to kill the Dominican Priuli, intending all the time to save him from the Sanmicheles. Toungeless, he knew it would be beyond his powers to explain such guile to Priuli's satisfaction. The role he plays in things is as ever a puzzle to me. I stop thinking about him, kiss Michaela, and go up on deck. Bad as the weather is, I prefer to be in the fresh air.

Occasionally we intercept fishing vessels coming from the east, hoping to gain intelligence of Ottoman naval movements. These sometimes carry refugees from Muslim devastated territories or even escaped Christians who have been enemy galley slaves, and these we interrogate at length. Then there are Greeks who hail the Fleet with the candid commercial intent of selling information, often ludicrous. These are the gentlemen mainly responsible for making the Christians think the Ottoman fleet is twice its real size, and the enemy think the same of ours.

In the lee of Cape Colonna we are forced to lie for three days in the absence of any inclination on the part of the Royal Galley to brave the gale that sweeps past the headland separating us from the Gulf of Taranto. In a fleet enduring such misfortune some of the blame might devolve upon the Commander-in-Chief since prudence and patience can be seen as lack of courage and skill by those already prejudiced against him for other reasons.

The Venetians loudly curse the day they allowed themselves to be taken to sea by a Spanish Archduke and a Papal Admiral: "only safe on his knees in church", and who never should have been permitted to imperil the ships and men upon which Venice depends for her very existence".

The arrogant soldiery take these expressions of contempt for Spain and the Church badly and scuffles break out when some of their officers are heard to speak slightingly of Venetian fighting qualities, particularly in relation to Cyprus.

"We Spaniards have been brought from the other end of the Mediterranean because you are letting the Muslims chase you out of Cyprus."

"You Venetians have become decadent and are no longer capable of defending yourselves."

Anti-Spanish feelings in all our ships are running high when Don John himself committed a rash act that brought snarls of contempt for Spain from the Venetians. Reports are received that some ships had been sighted and he believes he has found the Ottoman Fleet. Perhaps to redeem his reputation in the eyes of the Venetians he makes for the open sea at the head of thirty-five Spanish galleys notwithstanding the storm, only to find himself challenging our six gigantic Venetian galleasses. These have finally arrived to join us, and are late since they depend entirely on sail and, helpless in the headwinds, are being towed by galliots.

Then, on the afternoon of Friday, 21 September, a frigate from the east is blown around the cape and, after some hair-raising encounters with several galleys while her men are trying to get the sails off her, she anchors ahead of our Flagship. Her captain manages to board us by getting his men to pay out her anchor cable sufficiently to allow him to leap, at his life's risk, from his stern onto our ram, along which he clambers to Veniero who was waiting for him right forward. He hauls himself upright, grasping one of the forestays, and, when he has recovered his breath;

"Guido Cornaro, Admiral! I sailed from Corfu five days ago and have been looking for you with a message from the Provveditore of Corfu to say the Ottoman Fleet now lies under the walls of Prevesa. Ali Pasha is reported to have sent a frigate to Istanbul asking the Sultan whether he should stay and commit his fleet to battle with the Christians or whether he should withdraw to the Eastern Mediterranean."

Veniero clasps Cornaro's hand warmly;

"My friend, you have brought the news everyone is waiting for. I must now go over to the Royal Galley and tell Don John we can direct this fleet to Prevesa across the Ionian Sea without further delay. How do you estimate the distance?"

"About seventy leagues, Admiral."

Veniero orders his Galley Commander to select the most stalwart boat's crew. Opportunely, I noticed some squabble with the soldiery going on and absented myself from the group on the rambade. I lack courage, not courage to face swamping in the seas between us and the Royal Galley but courage to face Priuli who would of necessity be present at the meeting between Veniero and Don John.

The next morning I learn that the Archduke and his counsellors had not agreed with Veniero that the Allied Fleets should sail straight for Prevesa. They feel they cannot place too much reliance upon the report of the Venetian Provveditore of Corfu and furthermore they think it dangerous to commit the ships to the open sea whilst such weather persists. They think it safer to follow the Italian coastline as far as Taranto, and then to cross the Adriatic at its narrowest part from Otranto, so arriving at Corfu, then to cross to Prevesa. At this stage someone conveniently remembers that in the region of Otranto seven thousand more of the promised Christian infantry might be awaiting embarkation, a reinforcement that 'could not be overlooked'. This suggested pretext for another delay causes Veniero to rise in contempt and, leaving Don John without apologies, he makes his perilous boat trip back to the Venetian Flagship.

I lose no time in diving below deck to tell Michaela that we will be calling at Corfu, where she can at last go ashore to the safety and comfort of the Prefect's house. Corfu is a well-governed, civilized Venetian colony in constant communication with Venice. I seek out Marcantonio Sanmichele's letter to the Prefect. She jumps for joy and I have to tell her to keep her voice down.

She can barely contain her impatience as we lie under the headland of Cape Colonna all next day. When the tempest finally moderates on Saturday evening we cross the Gulf of Taranto, passing the point of Santa Maria di Leuca on Sunday. On Monday the weather is hot again; the Italian coast is behind us and in the afternoon I am able to go below and tell her Corfu is in sight, 'lying like a shield upon the misty deep', as Homer says. It transpires that he was referring to a Corfu of more innocent times.

CHAPTER EIGHTEEN

The eerie silence that greets our arrival at Corfu is explained when we enter that harbor of death. The advancing red line of blood and fire marking the surge of Muslim military might has passed through Corfu.

Tears well in veteran Venetian eyes as they survey the devastation. Strangled bodies of children are heaped with holy paintings that have been used as targets. Scimitar slashed Madonnas mingle with the half charred bodies of the old whose houses had been put to the torch. All others had been carried into slavery.

The initial ripples of pity and horror are followed by a common unspoken steeling of Venetian resolve to find and overcome the enemy. The effect on me is to plunge me into a well of self-condemnation, alleviated to some small extent by the labour of grave digging. Decomposing bodies threaten plague. The ships are anchored well clear of land and no one is allowed ashore except those Venetians, cloths tied around their mouths, who have volunteered to bury the dead. My mind turned in upon itself and I become my own enemy. So deep in deceit, I felt that I was deceiving my dedicated companions by daring to acquiesce even tacitly in their avowed war to the death, since my conscience couldn't reconcile this with the sacred oath I had taken. How could I be defending Michaela Sanmichele by taking her into a war to the death?

I clean myself as well as I can when I return on board and plan to tell Michaela only enough of what has happened to Corfu to make her understand that she has no hope of going ashore there. I dread the emotional scene that must follow, and think to ease things by pointing out that del Tacco's disobedience to her father's orders in refusing to call at Corfu has saved her from horrid death or the Istanbul Seraglio.

I find her already in tears for another reason: Murad has been dragged away from my cabin, and she has heard, from hiding, that he is to be flogged for absence from his place of duty on the rowing benches. She pleads with me to intercede for him, but how can I intervene? In any case the moment is highly inconvenient - Veniero is asking for me.

As I come up from our quarters, passing the rowing deck on the way to the Quarterdeck ladder, I see Murad lashed to the mainmast awaiting his punishment. I am annoyed with the way his eyes follow me like those of a dog betrayed, but I chase these imaginings from my mind.

But nothing is ever really erased from one's mind. At some level of my consciousness those eyes have followed me ever since. I ignored those eyes wilfully: I have paid for that deliberate act of wilfulness with much worse than death.

As soon as I arrive on the Quarterdeck Veniero notices me and orders me to stay there in case I am required. I take this as an admonishment for what he must consider as yet another inexplicable absence below decks. He has received dispatches from Venice, and stands surrounded by his officers reading them, passing them around with his usual informality. His own perusal is brief as he rapidly dismisses reams of Senatorial advice, and then he comes to a paragraph at which he halts and pales. He orders me to accompany him into his cabin

"Take a boat with this dispatch to Agostino Barbarigo's ship," he says weakly, "present my compliments to him and hand it to him, then ask him to come on board this Flagship. The Venetians must be told of the contents but I will ask him to tell them. At this time when strength is required they must not see their Commander-in-Chief in tears."

I take the dispatch across to Barbarigo's galley. Having looked it over, saying nothing, Barbarigo comes back to Veniero with me. On the way, he hands the papers to me to read and what I read will forever prey upon my mind.

The Muslim siege of the Venetian port of Farmagosta in Cyprus had by July - the report had been long in getting out of Cyprus - reduced the citizens to a state where they were eating dogs and horses. Hope of relief from the Venetian Navy having melted away the Governor, the valiant Marcantonio Bragadin, refused to subject the defenders and their wives and children to further suffering and sought and obtained what he thought were honourable surrender terms from Mustapha Pasha, the Ottoman Admiral.

Bragadin set out with his officers to hand over the city formally and was received by the Pasha with great courtesy. Then, so the astonishing report reads, the Pasha noticed amongst Bragadin's entourage an attractive young man, Antonio Querini. He demanded that Querini be handed over to him as a present. Bragadin refused since this had not formed any part of the conditions of surrender. The Pasha's courtesy was in seconds transformed into wrath so monstrous that volumes would not serve to relate the horror of the holocaust that followed.

While the manhood of the Farmagosta garrison was hunted out and flogged through the streets to galley chains, and the girls herded into transports for Istanbul and the Seraglio or lesser harems, the remainder were beheaded in oceans of blood. Bragadin had his nose and ears sliced off and was paraded through the Ottoman encampment daily on hands and knees with heavy sacks of earth suspended from his sides, and flogged into kissing the ground every time his circuit brought him before the Pasha's tent. On his seventeenth day of torment he was set in a pillory and flayed alive. His skin was then stuffed with straw and walked around the city on a donkey. Then it was put to hang from the main yardarm of Mustapha's galley.

Rage at their helplessness in the face of political pretexts for postponement of battle, bitter grief for their slaughtered kin; make for a black, black day in the Venetian galleys. When Don John summons the leaders to yet another conference on board the Royal Galley the Venetians ask in scornful wonderment what new grounds for loquacity the Spaniards might have found. Veniero orders me to accompany him and when we reach the head of Don John's gangway he pointedly hands me his sword to hold as he notices Gianandrea Doria, also arriving for the meeting. He is indicating to those present that he cannot trust himself not to use it on that prince. But for once a meeting was justified, as it turned out.

"We have received intelligence," proclaims the Archduke at the head of a table set on his Quarterdeck, "that the Ottoman Fleet has left Prevesa. We were misinformed when we were told Ali Pasha would lie there while his frigate collected instructions from Istanbul. We are given to believe that the Ottoman Fleet has now entered the Gulf of Corinth."

Doria stood up:" Most High Prince of Spain!" he begins, "Most Sacred Envoy of His Holiness the Pope! Princes of Mantova, Savoia,

Parma, Urbino, Toscana, Ferrara! You may today be so misguided as to lead this great Allied Fleet, so gloriously assembled, to an awful disaster, a disaster that will engulf the élite of the Nobility of Europe, for we are all present. Have we not heard that the Muslims used last winter to construct a formidable and integrated force that far outnumbers the combined Christian force, and which moreover owes allegiance to a single Prince, the Ottoman Sultan? Each of our squadrons, on the other hand, serves a different prince and some, such as the Venetians, serve no prince at all!"

"Consider, Princes, the favourable situation in which the enemy fleet now finds itself, if it has indeed come near to the entrance to the Gulf of Corinth. There it will be backed by a friendly hinterland. Overland routes from Istanbul terminate in such Muslim friendly bases as Patras and Lepanto, not to mention those deeper in that long, long gulf, all well founded in Ottoman held territory."

"Consider, Princes, whether we should not use our so arduously assembled forces where we are more certain of a victorious outcome!"

As the day wears on Prince after Prince rises to his feet to display his military competence in words. Scarcely the most miserable coastal enemy-defended heap of stones is too unimportant to deserve dreary debate as whether it might, or might not be a worthy target for the Allied Fleets. Veniero sits drumming his fingers on the ship's balustrade. When the Princes finished Barbarigo rises;

"Never more," he says, "Never again shall we find an opportunity so advantageous for bringing the enemy Fleet to battle. The whole tenor of the speeches we have heard today calls for discretion. I say that if ever there was a moment when daring is true discretion that moment is now. Caution at such a time can only be extreme rashness."

"Ours is the greatest force ever arrayed against the common enemy, and it is evident from the way in which Ali Pasha recedes before our advance that he is uncertain about the outcome of battle. This uncertainty springs from several sources: a large part of his Fleet must remain detached to hold down recent gains from Venice, amongst them Cyprus; his rowing benches are manned by shackled captives and ravaged by disease through denial of human decencies."

"I vow to God that after the sight of Corfu and this morning's news of the horror of Famagusta there is not one seaman from the Laguna who is not burning to avenge the Serenissima's cruel humiliation."

"Remember, Christian Princes, that we Venetians came to Messina to join your forces against our own wishes. Our desire in the summer was to sail straight for Cyprus. We came to Messina because the signatories of the Holy League, so our Senate tells us, have resolved to combine forces to sweep the Muslim from the Mediterranean. We know that they will only be cleared from the Mediterranean when the Ottoman Fleet is destroyed."

"Had we not acceded to the appeal of His Holiness to join you rather than sail for Cyprus as we intended we should not, each one of us, have to live with the nightmare of Farmagosta, a nightmare from which we can never wake up."

CHAPTER NINETEEN

Barbarigo's reasoning prevails over Doria's eloquence and the assembled Princes at last agree that the Allied Fleets will move south hoping that Ali Pasha, commanding the Ottoman Fleet, is bottled up inside the Gulf of Corinth. But first Don John thinks it necessary to decree a Fleet Inspection. The ships are to be reviewed in the formation that they are to take up before battle.

To carry out this inspection since it means that two hundred galleys, not counting the reserve are required to lie in line abreast a vast protected bay is needed. The Bay of Igominitza six leagues to the southeast of Corfu is chosen. Here the fleets can lie under the shelter of the Mainland Mountains that will mitigate the force of the dangerous north and northeast wind.

We moved into the warmth of late summer as the galleys slide through smooth seas towards their designated points of anchorage in that wide bay. Warm weather brings with it gregariousness, although subdued. No longer are Michaela and I screened from the world by the isolating self-interest that foul weather imposes on the individual. People begin to take an inconvenient interest in each other. Nevertheless whenever exposure threatens somehow Murad manages to put himself between Michaela and the outside world without drawing attention either to himself or her and I am able to go about my duties, if not with an easy mind at least feeling I could leave her in relative safety. But now I am haunted by a new fear. I am ignorant of what is meant by 'Inspection' and the word fills me with apprehension. Will every compartment in every ship be visited? Then, preoccupied as I am Murad's bitter eyes cause me an uneasiness that eludes definition.

We are the last to leave Corfu since Veniero has still to carry out some acts of mercy for the stricken island so we arrive in the bay when all the other galleys are already anchored. Rather than unsettle the formation Veniero chooses to anchor not far from the entrance to the bay. The drift of the current there is such that it sets the Flagship of Venice broadside on to the rest of the assembled fleets. This position, near the open sea, appeals to Veniero as symbolic of the resentment he feels at once more having to remain in harbor on yet another pretext, instead of chasing the Ottoman.

Don John of Austria carries out the first part of the Inspection on the following morning, passing down the lines of galleys in a frigate accompanied by his Chief of Staff, the Grand Admiral Requesens. Gunners and musketeers acquit themselves to the Commander-in-Chief's satisfaction except that, in saluting him with supposedly blank fire a musketeer from one of the galleys shoots and kills a man in Don John's entourage.

Twenty lives have been lost by musket fire since leaving Messina either through carelessness or downright mischief. Several times Don John has issued orders intended to prevent this kind of thing and now he proclaims it an offence that must be punished by hanging the musketeer to blame. He sends dispatch vessels down the line announcing this. At the same time it is declared that the commander of any galley where this offence occurs will be tried and punished if found guilty of negligence in administering this new law. I am seized with dismay when I learn that additionally an internal inspection of the galleys will be carried out in the afternoon by officers designated by the Archduke.

In the afternoon Veniero, as senior officer of the Venetian forces, prepares to receive Don John on board the Flagship of Venice. He naturally expects no lesser person to subject his ship to internal inspection. Veniero commands us to see that the ship is particularly smart and squared off and that the men are cleanly turned out and assembled in an orderly fashion. Perhaps he thinks of this as an occasion for reconciliation with Don John after so many unfortunate disagreements; he may also see it as an opportunity for discussion of the tactics the approaching battle will employ.

In the late afternoon, long prepared and waiting on the Quarterdeck to receive Don John, Veniero's sharp eyes detect the standard of Gianandrea Doria at the masthead of an approaching boat. At first he is incredulous. Then, his lips set hard in decision, he sharply orders his Galley Commander to hoist the galley's gangway and the officers to get themselves below deck. He follows them. Unable to board, Gianandrea Doria circles the Flagship of Venice, loudly and peevishly addressing those in sight, mainly the rowers;

"As representative of the Archduke, brother of His Holy Majesty the King of Spain, I will not be treated in this way!"

This brings ribald laughter from Venetian sailors on deck because evidently he is being so treated. When, after circuiting the ship twice, he realizes that Veniero will not receive him he withdraws hurling threats over the stern of his boat.

Over an hour later the Grand Admiral Requesens comes. The gangway is lowered and he is received by Veniero coldly. He gives a rapid and superficial glance over the Flagship, not even going below deck, and departs with the minimum of cordiality.

CHAPTER TWENTY

The bay is exceptionally still in the approaching evening. The wash of the boat carrying the departing Requesens dies away and not a breath of wind stirs the glassy surface. Then, as the Grand Admiral's boat disappears amongst the galleys some shots ring out.

"Some musketeer is saluting him," a sailor is heard to jest.

"Hope he remembers to load with ball," quipped another.

But Veniero, listening carefully, points in a different direction to where, towards the north side of the bay, lie some Cretan galleys, part of Veniero's command. There comes across the calm water faint shouting and further shots. After some minutes of quiet we see a small boat detach itself from the line of galleys and come towards us in haste. As it comes alongside we see that it is manned by a lone and aged sailor. He makes his boat fast and mounts our still lowered gangway breathlessly;

"Pardon, my Lord," he exclaims, surprised at being immediately confronted by his Commander-in-Chief at the top of the gangway.

"What's going on in those galleys?" demands Veniero.

"It's the Spanish soldiery, my Lord. They are at blows with us Venetians. Shots have been fired and there are dead."

"And what is your Galley Commander doing about it?"

"Signor Calergi sent me to get help, my Lord. He cannot bring the galley under control because the Captain of Militia has reviled us. He says that Farmagosta fell because we Venetians did not have the courage to take our ships there and drive the Muslims away but came to Messina looking for protection from the other fleets."

Sebastiano Veniero looks around and finds me at his elbow;

"Take a party of men Valente and arrest this Captain of Militia in my name and any other malefactors and bring them before me. Galley Commander, prepare a boat and four good men to accompany Valente - when he has got his armour on."

I dive down the ladder to our cabin to prepare myself. Michaela unbolts the door at the sound of my voice.

"Where's Murad," I ask, casting off my outer clothes. I need his help with my armour."

"He needed your help when they flogged him! Is the battle coming now?"

"No, my love," I reply, struggling with the pieces, "there is no danger for you. I am simply being sent to another galley to arrest a mutineer."

"There is danger for you then?"

"I see no danger."

"No? You never see danger! Can you not see that your immortal soul is in danger? God will punish us, you and me, for our sins."

"Sins? Michaela, there is a boat waiting for me! I have told you that we have committed no sin. The Church cannot fail to marry us when this is over, and we will be forgiven."

"It's not THAT," says Michaela. "I have prayed for guidance and now I understand that what our bodies do together is not sin as long as our thoughts are holy."

"I wish you would not always talk about sin, Michaela."

I am impatient, knowing that they are waiting for me on deck.

"Marco, I love you and I am afraid for the danger to your immortal soul more than I am afraid for your life. You are too curious about things that the Holy Church does not wish us to know," she whispers uncertainly, her head down and her arms embracing me.

"But where do you get these ideas from? What things do you mean?"

"I mean those Classical texts you spoke about that evening when the Loredans were having supper with us."

"Who told you that it was wrong to talk about them?"

Naturally it has been the young Loredan, I think, and wonder why that stupid man has so much influence over her. But no! It wasn't Loredan. Her answer made me momentarily forget my mission and all around me.

"Priuli - the Inquisitor - said it when he came to see my father - the morning before my father asked you to take me away."

A few seconds pass before I find the words;

"But Priuli!" After the way he behaved!" How could you worry about what a man like that says?"

"I know he has failings as a man, Marco, but he was speaking in his sacred role as the Inquisitor sent to us from Rome, not as just a man. He said God would punish you."

These were almost the last words I heard from Michaela. The Galley Commander's call for me came closer and his steps sound on the ladder. I must not be caught with her - and at such a time! I shout that I am coming, give Michaela a light kiss, and whisper to her not to concern her pretty head with nonsense and to keep herself well hidden. Taking up my sword I join my four men waiting in the boat.

As we approach the Cretan galley I expect that the sight of the Admiral's standard at the masthead of the boat, indicating Veniero's intervention, will bring order amongst the ruffians before I have to board. In the event, when I do board I find that the situation is indeed well out of control. The Venetian officers and sailors have all been driven to the fore part of the ship, while the Spanish soldiery stand along port and starboard gunwales pointing their musketry at them. Amidships, his broad and bloodstained shoulders bent as he is releasing a halyard, the Spanish Captain of Militia turns his head to greet my appearance with feigned amusement,

"Boy!" he yells, fixing me with a maniacal eye, "Boy, I have taken command of this vessel and am about to haul down the Venetian flag."

The lout filled me with loathing, and trepidation. But all Venetian eyes were on me. I descend to the rowing deck and advance towards him, sword drawn. Time seemed to slow down and I feel split into two entities, one the unwilling hero, the other watching me making a fool of myself. Muzio Alticozzi, for I learned afterwards that this was his despicable name and that he is notorious for his filthy tongue amongst those whose misfortune it is to incur his foul-mouthed offensiveness, does not even condescend to draw his sword against me. Curling his lip in contempt he smashes down my sword arm with a heavy chain I have not noticed since he has it in his left hand behind him. At the same instant I am caught from behind by a musket ball that slams into the left pauldron of my armour, opening up the interstices. Shocked and sick I fall backwards ingloriously across some rowing benches.

In the long seconds that I lie there shame drenched my mind. Expecting to face mockery when I raise my head instead I heard a thunderous stampede. The Venetian sailors and rowers had taken heart at my advance upon Alticozzi and now come in an avalanche upon him. Many Venetians are injured by his furious sword and chain attack but several overpower him and the rowers attack the musketeers low and swiftly, plunging the gunwale-mounted soldiery into the sea, since a soldier is easily unbalanced in a ship.

I am helped to my feet and since Alticozzi is being held disabled manage to recover some dignity by continuing his task of hauling on the ensign halyard to bind the brute. It is the most easily available means by which the rowers can secure him. With it inevitably comes the Venetian ensign which also went tight-bound around his body in the tussle to lash him up well. Alticozzi thrashes away unceasingly mouthing insults so I lay the point of my sword at his throat to quieten him.

*I am to take you before the Admiral of Venice."

"I spit upon the flag of Venice!"

So saying he heaves his head up and spits upon the Lion flag unhappily caught in his lashings. I withdraw the point of my sword slightly since it is not my mission to kill the prisoner, and this brings from him a further stream of derision. My men lift him and bear him to the gangway. Having captured him, and seeing that Calergi is regaining control of his galley I feel I have achieved enough and forget that I have been ordered to arrest his accomplices as well. But in the odd way that things go in military life three companions follow him into captivity.

On pausing at the gangway I have the presence of mind to ask Calergi to let me have some witnesses of the evening's events from his ship's company. These he supplies and he also supplies a second boat since we are overloaded. The journey back to the Flagship seemed long. The pain and coldness in my left shoulder, not noticed in the warmth of the furore, begins to make itself felt. Blood flows down my arm and stiffens in my palm and between my fingers. I suppose the current is against us for the Flagship seems never to get any nearer, her masts and shrouds skeletal against the evening sky.

I am unprepared for the excessively martial attitude that my four men suddenly assume when we come within hailing distance. As we come alongside they manhandle the bound and ranting Alticozzi with studied inconsideration, hounding the other prisoners up the gangway at dagger point. From the crowded gunwhales the Venetians bawl approbation and, as I go on board, an unofficial salutation from an admiring trumpeter makes me uncomfortably aware of unearned glory.

My men will not, I know, recount my ignoble scuffle with Alticozzi. They can hardly do so and still enjoy acclaim as the bloodstained vanquishers of savage mutineers. Sometime in the future

I will have to explain it all to the other officers and to Veniero. But not now. It can wait until I feel strong enough to relate the story properly. Veniero's surgeon comes forward and makes me lie down on one of the Quarterdeck lockers under the stern lantern and dismantles my armour and cuts away the under sleeve. The bound militia captain is laid writhing on the planks of the Quarterdeck and his men are lined up near him. Sebastiano Veniero addresses him;

"Who are you?"

"My name is Muzio Alticozzi. I am a Captain of the Spanish Infantry and I spit upon your flag."

So saying the beast heaves himself up and spits and slimy spittle runs over the Lion ensign caught in his bonds. Veniero characteristically and slowly unbuckles his sword belt and hands his sword into the safekeeping of the Galley Commander who stands by him. He asks Alticozzi's supporters what has happened and they enthusiastically relate what their master was engaged in and how many men he killed and injured. Veniero looks down at Alticozzi;

"So you are a mutineer and a murderer and these men are your accomplices?"

"You say so. I see it differently."

"How, may I ask?"

"The King of Spain's brother, Don John, has placed us in your galleys to see that you fight and don't run away as you Venetians are accustomed to. Why didn't you take your galleys to Farmagosta? Why come expecting the King's galleys to do your work for you? They were your people, weren't they? Release us and send us back with an apology, and the consequences from Don John may not be so severe for you."

"Murder and mutiny in one of the Republic's ships of war!"

Veniero brings out the words slowly, keeping control of himself,

"Rarely are such heinous crimes confessed so lightly."

Veniero looks into the faces of his officers and sees that there can be no alternative. He orders the main yard to be lowered and four nooses rigged along it. Then he has it rehoisted to a convenient height above the centre gangway, and a keg placed under each noose. Lengths of rope are bighted around the lower part of the kegs. Thrashing and pleading, threatening and howling, Alticozzi and the four are strung up. On a sharp word of command sailors haul the kegs from under them and the mutineers swing free to a prolonged roll on the drums.

CHAPTER TWENTY-ONE

Someone has draped a heavy cloak over me to keep off the chill that comes with late evening. Deep red floods the western sky, and remembering the skeletal appearance of the ship as we approached her earlier on as she stood alone against the setting sun at the entrance to the bay, the horrid thought crossed my mind that to the fleets of the assembled nations our evening's work must look, in the blood red sunset, like four rabbits on a spit dangling over the mouth of Hell.

Veniero has gone to his quarters having told the surgeon that it was not necessary to carry me below which would have meant negotiating difficult ladders, at least not until we had to sail when I could not be left on the weather deck. A silence has fallen over the entire Allied Fleets. I am glad that Michael who would be worried about my wound, of which all must know, had the sense not to come near me.

Half-an-hour goes by, then in the stillness I sense rather than hear movement near the ship as boats began to creep closer, and then even closer by those requiring further confirmation of what their eyes told them. When hailed, as is the custom when a boat approaches, they withdraw hastily. After a further interval I heard a splash of oars under the starboard gangway and Ludovico Priuli's baldhead, glinting redly in the departing day, appears above the parapet. He stands at the ship's entrance and, crossing himself, holds up his large wooden crucifix towards the dangling bodies and begins to intone prayers.

"What brings you here?" Veniero is already at the top of the ladder to block Priuli's way further into the ship.

"I am commanded by Prince Colonna, the Papal Admiral, in my capacity as liaison officer with the Venetians to obtain from you a report on these executions." His eyes turn to the swinging corpses.

"Colonna!*Do I now come under Colonna's command?"

"Prince Colonna is interceding with His Highness, the Archduke, on your behalf, Admiral. Archduke Don John has been made aware that you have hanged an officer of the Spanish Militia and he takes this as the grossest insult to his royal brother, His Most Catholic Majesty of Spain. His counsellors are pressing him to hang you as you have hanged that officer. Prince Colonna has prevailed upon the Archduke to hear your case. That is where the matter stands at the moment. You must understand that Prince Colonna is pleading on your behalf since it is his function as the highest military officer of His Holiness the Pope to mediate and keep peace amongst the Christian nations."

"Colonna would have an easier task if the Spaniards could be persuaded not to lead mutinies and commit murders on board my galleys. Since you are the liaison officer I would have thought it your duty to present the Venetian case."

"That I can only do if I am supplied with the facts. Were these men given a fair trial?"

"Trial!* they convicted themselves out of their own mouths in front of my officers and men. They boasted of their crimes. Should I have limited myself to collecting their confessions and to handing them over to Don John for trial by a Court Martial appointed by him, giving the Spaniards an excuse to remain in harbor for a further week? So far when I have attempted to draw attention to criminal acts by Spanish Militia these have been returned to their ships without punishment as an indication of the ease with which my authority can be flouted. As well as the duty of bringing my ships to fight the Muslims I have the responsibility of upholding the dignity of Venice before the world. I should hardly be doing this were I to allow riff-raff to revile the name of the Serenissima on the Quarterdeck of Her Flagship and live. At Messina Don John hanged two of our men for something as harmless as blasphemy!"

The Dominican put his hands to his ears to shut out such impiety.

"The Archduke Don John will probably not accept your reasoning."

"It satisfies me. Now that I have finally dragged the Spaniards to battle I intend to see that Venetian galleys are commanded by Venetian officers when we meet the Ottoman, not roughneck soldiery imposed upon them by your friends the Spaniards. Now, go monk! Never board a Venetian ship again while I am in command."

Ludovico Priuli hesitates at the top of the gangway then turning and crossing himself again he descends into his boat not having noticed, I mistakenly think, who lies on the Quarterdeck locker.

As darkness closes the bodies are cut down, weighted with shot, and dropped overboard. Veniero orders the yardarm to be trimmed ready for sea and boats are sent to the other Venetian galleys conveying his orders for the night: that all Venetian galleys are to be ready to put to sea on his orders and that the signal to sail will be nothing other than the motion of his dimmed stern lantern as the Flagship leaves the bay. The other Venetian galleys are to remain with their lanterns unlit as they slide from their anchorages in order to minimize attention and the chance of a Spanish attack upon them, which he now fears.

I doze for a long time during the comings and goings occasioned by the transmission of these orders and I awake to find Michaela's hand in mine. She has crept up from below and lies in the shadow between the locker and the balustrade. Becoming fully conscious I push away the cloak and struggled to get up. Stiff now, and my bruises hardened, slowly and painfully I lift myself to a sitting position and have hardly done so when I hear another boat approaching. I lower and cover myself. Hope that we could remain undiscovered drains away fast when I heard Veniero confronting the arrivals - Prince Colonna followed by Priuli.

"May I inquire as to why Your Highness offends me by bringing this monk with you? I have told him he is not welcome in any of the Republic's warships."

"Admiral of Venice, you have imperilled the Holy Alliance by taking it upon yourself to execute subjects of His Most Catholic Majesty, King Philip of Spain and you have offended the Archduke himself."

"Have you not told your masters," Veniero demands patiently of Priuli, "that these men convicted themselves of mutiny before me and my officers and have suffered the penalty usually inflicted on mutineers in ships of war?"

The Dominican was not listening. He was standing over me.

"Yes, it IS our Classical Scholar! Do YOU remember ME, Valente?"

"Leave that boy in peace, monk! He has served the Republic well today."

"He is one whose immortal soul may be in peril through courting dangerous heresies, Your Highness!" Priuli addresses Colonna, then he falls to his knees, and starts praying loudly. My mind, struggling to understand the Dominican's goes back to Paolo Loredan's mockery on the day we lunched on Augusto Contarini-Colonna's galley.

I cannot be certain of the sequence of events from there on. I think delirium has set in and the voices sound strange. Perhaps it is a sob from the darkness down behind the locker that makes the monk get to his feet and look closer, and perhaps he already knew whom he would find there. I think that suspicion of Michaela's presence on board might have been communicated to him by Paolo Loredan, who could have received a letter from someone malicious in Venice while we lay at Corfu.

Now Veniero is giving attention to what Priuli is shouting.

"Senator Sanmichele's daughter?* Monk, you have taken leave of your senses?"

"It is true, Admiral." I strive to admit, but I suppose my voice was weak for no one seemed to hear me.

"Here, out you come!" Priuli dragged Michaela in front of Veniero and Colonna. "Take off your clothes, and then perhaps they will believe me."

I hear Michaela whisper something that must have been a plea admitting guilt so as to be spared from having to strip off her clothes. Anyway it couldn't have been difficult to see that she is a girl ill disguised as a boy servant. All along, only the fact that she was locked in my cabin had kept her sex secret from the rest of those in the ship, except of course Murad. Perhaps even Veniero recognizes her, now that his attention is drawn to her, from seeing her at her home in Venice on the occasions that Sanmichele entertained him.

"The heretic, Valente, has profaned the Holiness of our expedition against the Ottoman." Priuli clamours, while Veniero gives orders to the Galley Commander as to how Michaela is to be looked after.

Michaela's shame is most satisfactory to Priuli. If before he had a hold on Marcantonio Sanmichele, blackmailing him over accepting money from the French, how much more power would he have now that he could reveal, if he chose, that Sanmichele had abandoned his daughter to heresy and promiscuity. Now he could show the world meritorious grounds for taking charge of her. So in attempting to rescue her I had strengthened his hand. Sanmichele would continue to be threatened by Priuli who could through him apply leverage on the Venetian Senate in favour of the Inquisitorial policy of the Holy See.

When they have arranged the fate of my poor Michaela they turn to other important matters;

"There is a charge almost as serious as heresy I wish to bring against Valente. He tried to murder me!"

Veniero almost smiles;

"How?* were you in the affray on board the Cretan galley this afternoon?"

"No, of course not.* this was in Venice."

"Then it shall be investigated in Venice, after the battle."

"But you have a witness here on board - Valente's servant Murad - and he will tell you how he identified Valente - by means of the green doublet which Valente wore on the night of the attempt, which was later found near the scene."

How does Priuli know this, I wonder. He must have been in touch with Murad all along.

"Leave us, monk! Do you think this is a time to be discussing green doublets?"

I am thinking battle will come and I may die with these accusations levelled against me; heresy, incest and attempted murder of the Liaison Officer! Falsely, the afternoon's skirmish has gained me temporary favour in the eyes of the powerful Veniero. Could real success in battle, when it comes, ensure his continued favour? How I pray for success in battle!

"I am charged by His Holiness, the Pope, to maintain peace between the nations here gathered to fight the Ottoman," Prince Colonna is saying. "I find it a hard task, Admiral of Venice, in the face of your widely known arrogance and obstinacy. We cannot let the Alliance fall apart, and yet how is the Archduke to accept the Venetian behaviour of this night?" He is back to the executions.

"He will accept it as best he may until he grows up and learns through experience."

"Admiral of Venice, if you maintain this stubborn attitude the Holy Alliance will be destroyed tonight. The Spaniards will attack your ships. Let me suggest to you a compromise that may be acceptable to His Royal Highness. Let us admit that the young man on the locker has today played a significant part in worsening the already unhappy relationships between our nations. Why should we, the responsible veterans, suffer through the rash activities of these hot-blooded youngsters - and we see how hot-blooded he is indeed!" His eyes followed Michaela as she was being taken forward to some rambade compartment of the vessel.

"I am obliged to give credence to the word of this Holy Friar," continued Colonna, turning again to Veniero, "that this same young man may have committed certain acts which could be deemed heresy and, for the benefit of his immortal soul he should be examined by an appointed Court of Inquisition, a trial which we cannot undertake now in view of our state of war. Let us say that I, as the highest military authority under His Holiness the Pope, have commanded him to appear at a later date before a Court of the Holy Inquisition, and meanwhile that you, Admiral of Venice, have justly consigned him to me to be imprisoned on board the Papal Galley as a result of the part that he has played in causing a rift in our Alliance, and until the charge of attempted murder brought by the Liaison Officer, Priuli, can be investigated."

His words and not Priuli's shock me into realizing that others might, with justification, think me guilty of trying to kill the monk. That Priuli thought it was I who had tried to murder him meant he had not seen the face of his attacker that night. Nicolò must have sneaked up on him from behind and his suspicion that it was I was reinforced by Murad's identification of that wretched green doublet. He would not have found it difficult to believe that I wanted to kill him, having a few hours earlier that evening in the Sanmichele's house almost pierced him with my dagger. Understandably he felt his life insecure as long as I was free. I was very relieved to hear Admiral Veniero say;

"Valente will not be consigned anywhere by me except to the sick quarters in this ship, and there he will be under guard. I know nothing of this alleged murder attempt, or of heresies. Galley Commander, call the surgeon and ask him to have Valente taken below. It is getting cold here on deck."

"Since you are so difficult I must report to the Archduke that I have left this Holy Friar in charge of Valente. I pray that you will accept this compromise. I can think of no other solution. Priuli may be considered appropriate since it is his duty to liaise between His Highness and the Venetians."

"Your monk may stay on board this ship. Indeed I can hardly refuse seeing that he has been made our Liaison Officer and so my Flagship is his place of duty, but he is not to go near Valente. I am weary of this bickering. Goodnight!"

"In days or hours," said Colonna, pausing at the head of the gangway to make the sign of the cross before he goes to his boat, "we hope to be committed to a battle on which the survival of Christendom depends. I trust that when the time comes to make our victorious report we will find grounds in Venetian valour in battle to warrant pardoning this day's disloyalties."

CHAPTER TWENTY-TWO

Reveillé sounded before dawn this morning. The stars are still bright. It is three days since we left Igominitza. Here at last we meet Ali Pasha and the enemy fleet.

Today we shall see battle! says the surgeon as he helps me fit on my armour, now releasing me from his quarters from which all, especially Priuli, have been excluded on Veniero's express orders. Terror of Priuli? Then dread that some, perhaps all of my fellows, Venetians and Capodistrians will be bleeding and even dying within the hour. After the battle? Well! I think that after the battle Priuli or I or both of us may be dead. Worry about Michaela? But she is locked away safely in the Admiral's quarters.

I am distressed for all and everything that this day may bring. After the battle if we survive the only thing Priuli can do worse for her than he has already done is to kill me, by poison or some other cowardly means. Here on board the Venetian Flagship he can do nothing to me, at least not without helpers. Where will he find these? Not amongst the Venetians!

Often I have wondered how I would behave in battle and as often have brushed aside the thought. Within minutes the awful finality of knowing must arrive. Here in the surgeon's quarters his curiously shaped knives haunt the mind with thoughts of the softness and transience of human flesh. But I am grateful to the surgeon. My fever has gone and my left shoulder although stiff now serves my arm well. Occasionally I feel a stab of pain. I think that perhaps a splinter of the metal from my smashed shoulder piece is embedded there.

Out on deck under the wide and cloudless skies East and West are closing on each other in glorious pageantry drugging the senses with dreams of glory. As the grey dawn changes to gold we become aware that we are being hailed by one of the galleasses. Glancing where they are indicating we see two strange sails tipping the horizon.

Veniero sends the man with the keenest eyes on board to the masthead to report and this man bellows down news of another and another and another sail and soon we see the increasingly sharp line of the eastern horizon dentated by the Turkish fleet. Ali Pasha's ships form an immense crescent stretching from shore to shore of the straits. The Ottoman right wing facing the Venetian left wing of our Fleet appears to consist of at least sixty galleys and so is evenly matched with ours. If reports prove true, it is commanded by Mahomet Sirocco, Pasha of Alexandria. We know that Ali Pasha himself is in command of the great preponderance of galleys forming the centre whilst Al Ali should be commanding the Ottoman left wing to the south.

The wind has been blowing from the east, the prevailing wind for October, capping the islands with cloud and the sea is running high. But the range between the fleets is closing and the waves are sinking to a glassy smoothness. The wind is shifting to the west so that the Turks have to toil hard at the oars, while our ships are advancing happily towards them on a light breeze. Even so the Turks have a disposition advantage from which they can bring all their ships into battle, which forces Don John to alter the course of our entire centre and right wing to allow our left to clear the shallow waters of the coastal region.

In the centre are Don John's sixty-four galleys, Don John in the Royal Galley flanked by us in the Venetian Flagship on his port side, and Marcantonio Colonna in the Papal Flagship on his starboard. The center consists of Spanish and Venetian galleys whilst the right wing is formed of Papal and Genoese galleys under Gianandrea Doria and the left wing is Venetian, commanded by Barbarigo. Astern of us is a reserve of thirty-five galleys under the Marquis of Santa Cruz and ahead the Venetian galleasses.

These six Venetian galleasses, or great galleys, are being towed, each by two galliots, to their positions about a mile ahead of the main line of battle. Two are placed before each of the three main divisions of the fleet. Gigantic and with exceptional firepower, they seem solid as floating fortresses in contrast to the long lines of slender galleys. Command of these has been retained for members of the great Venetian patrician families, so I have learnt since my more ingenuous days when I dared, in a wild moment, to ask for command of one of them. Commanders of these are expected to make a vow to take on single handed as many as twenty-five enemy galleys should occasion demand it. The two galleasses standing before our wing are commanded by Antonio Bragadin and Ambrosio Bragadin, brothers, each burning to avenge the family name so hideously defamed at Farmagosta.

Closer still now Turkish banners and insignia become distinguishable and the splendour and colour of the brilliant dress of the Janissaries with their tall crests and lavish plumes. Shouting to us to advance and be slaughtered, the Ottoman are dancing and clanging their arms, blowing trumpets, clashing cymbals and discharging volleys of musketry, useless because we are still well out of range.

From the far left we see that Barbarigo has sent a fast craft along the line to correct defects in alignment. In the Flagship and in the other galleys we hear the arquebusiers, musketeers and bombardiers, being instructed to make a final careful check of their weapons and equipment and to stand to their posts. Soldiers continue to sharpen the already faultless edges of their pikes and cutlasses and we galley officers balance our swords mock-heroically in our palms.

Now, following the example of the Royal Galley, a Cross is raised to the masthead of every ship in the Fleet. The Royal Galley itself advances some ship's lengths ahead of the line of battle, and in the bows Don John kneels in prayer, his officers standing clear and leaving him alone and conspicuous in full and glinting armour. The tens of thousands he commands quietly fall to their knees; the rowers at their benches, the soldiers on the bulwarks, the gunners with firebrands ready beside their guns. In each galley Dominicans or Franciscans in black or brown gowns hold aloft crucifixes and sprinkle holy water, promising absolution and pardon to all who fight valiantly this day. Devotions ended we stand to our posts each galley's side agleam with armour, helmets, pikes, swords and breastplates blazing in the early morning sun.

All eyes now turn to the Royal Galley at the report of one of its heavy cannon. We see the pre-arranged signal for battle, a square green ensign broken at the main peak. And at her masthead appears a previously unhoisted, specially prepared standard of the Holy League - a vast blue damask square embroidered in gold with Christ Crucified and the arms of Venice, the Pope, Spain and Don John. The trumpeters sound the charge and a flash appears from the bows of one of the galleasses, all six of which in seconds are pouring murderous fire into the Turkish centre and the right wing. Ottoman vessels struck seem arrested in their course as though brought up hard against a wall of steel. Ali Pasha is clearly trying to avoid this devastating barrage, thrusting his galleys directly at the Christian galleys and attempting to circumvent the galleasses, but in trying to do this he breaks his own battle line. The result for the enemy is chaos.

The enormous destruction of ships and men inflicted by the fire-power of the galleasses is plain for all to see and the evident destruction of Ottoman morale brings joy to Venetian hearts. But as the enemy galleys engage with Christian the great guns of the galleasses can no longer isolate their targets and they fall silent except for occasionally firing at stragglers. Arquebusiers and archers come into their own and galley rams galley, galley's cannon firing at point blank range into galleys' rowing deck and ship's side. The battle is fast becoming a series of unrelated struggles where organized naval tactics give way to individual skill and courage.

Mahomet Sirocco, the Pasha of Alexandria, has succeeded in clearing his right wing of the galleasses. He now tries to pass between the Venetian left wing and the shore, probably hoping to cause confusion by attacking from astern and breaking up the carefully held line formation. It is here that the Capodistrian Leona is fifteenth of the fifty-three galleys in that wing.

Barbarigo prepares to oppose this circumvention by adopting the same tactics, but his ships are in danger in the shoal waters. The Christian line breaks and Barbarigo's galley disappears into the midst of a dozen or so of the enemy, deluged by cannon, musketry and arrows, which the enemy are beginning to use extensively. Venetian ships converge to Barbarigo's rescue. Formation is broken and we are close enough for our cannon to sweep the decks of his principal opponent, scattering the enemy ranks and allowing us to board and advance foot by foot across the blood-slippery decks of a galley our prize and, as Flagship, we call upon another craft to take it in tow.

Smoke from the deadly Greek-fire ships erupts into roaring infernos as escaping Ottoman galleys throw torches into them and set them adrift. More smoke begins to shroud the surface of the sea rendering the enemy less easily identifiable, and noise rather than sight indicates where battles are raging. Enemy yells of encouragement mean trouble somewhere on our port bow so we alter course and come to Barbarigo's galley, still hard pressed. Coming near we see Barbarigo, a conspicuous figure on his Quarterdeck. His ship's woodwork is studded with arrows. It is hardly conceivable that he has so far survived this hail of death - and now he falls, an arrow through his face. Canale takes over the galley as Barbarigo is carried below.

Augusto Contarini-Colonna's galley appears through a veil of smoke and Augusto falls wounded as he leads his men to Canale's support. Many brave men have fallen, but enemy weight of numbers can't prevail against the resolute Venetian thirst for vengeance. Officers and men have even removed their helmets the better to see and kill. The Ottoman spearhead loses the initiative as Mahomet Sirocco's galley is sunk by Canale who, depressing his cannon to minimum elevation by sending all the men he can spare to the fore part of the ship, fires into the Muslim galley's side. We pick Mahomet Sirocco, Pasha of Alexandria, out of the water.

The sway of battle is carrying the Venetian galleys towards the northern shore, where hard pressed Muslims are abandoning their ships in shallow water and taking to land, only to be followed on shore by those who slay them as they attempt to take cover amongst rocks. But as the fumes of guns and fires begin to close in on us, the overall view of the battle is lost, and our interest is forced inwards on our immediate surroundings. Enemy galleys are burning around us unignited fire ships float past, those released on us by the Ottoman at the outset of battle. The waves are red with blood from broken limbs of suspended corpses, and strewn with spars, masts, cabin furniture, rich clothing and rags. If a wounded foe utters a feeble cry for help he is answered with musket shot. A badly injured Muslim has been found hiding under our rowing benches and is saved from further misery when someone slices off his head.

After helping to carry the wounded Galley Commander below I race up onto the rambade deck, sword waving, for another encounter. With matted bloody hair and armour wet with blood I must be a sight to freeze the sap of the enemy in his veins. I grab an axe from its housing at the foot of the main mast and hurl myself forward waving it in the faces of Murad and Priuli who are together in the bows Then I stumble and go down like a pole-axed beast, struck in the left femur by a ball fired from somewhere in the smoke. No pain at first! I am struggling to rise but my left leg lies out to the side as though it forms no part of me. Veniero and the other officers are all fighting on the quarterdeck at the other end of the ship – out of sight. Murad swiftly lashes me to a spar. Is this to carry me to safety without disturbing further my bones? He takes the feet end of the spar and I follow his eyes to see who carries the head end.....

"He knows! Gag him," yells Priuli, dropping the spar and tearing off the hanging part of one of his long black Dominican sleeves, which the powerful Murad is rapidly making into a tight ball, forcing it into my mouth. Michaela whom I have not seen since we were separated at Igominitza, is dragging at Priuli's arm, but he flings her back. An axe lies close by me. I manage to grasp it, frantic to cut away the bow rope of one of the unignited fire ships, drifting close, which Priuli and Murad are making fast to our galley. I read their minds with horror, but I am too bound and too weak to aim the axe properly and it is too late to cut the rope so that the evil fire ship can drift astern before they get me onto it and ignite it. But they can't release my grip from the axe so it comes with me.

Although discarded weapons are lying all around I know that Priuli will not kill or beat me unconscious before consigning me to the fire. He won't strangle me. An unrepentant heretic must die by fire and Priuli's fanaticism will not let him hear any repentance from me that might reprieve me. He has gagged me to prevent this more than to muffle my cries that wouldn't have been heard anyway above the noise of battle. Taking up the whole weight of the spar to which I am bound Murad leaps into the fire ship, and is now lashing the spar with me on it to the crude iron fire basket. Hurling himself back on board the galley he throws a burning gun torch into the fire ship to ignite it and casts off the fire ship's line. As I drift away I can see Priuli and Michaela kneeling together on the Flagship's foredeck, their arms held up to smoky skies...and the axe is slipping from my hands........

CHAPTER TWENTY-THREE

In May 2005 Professor Papazaglou of the Athenian Heritage Trust Was cruising along the northern coast of the Gulf of Corinth and at Perachora he came across a short fresh water canal which he entered and he found himself in a above the sandy bottom. On the aboutstood the ruins of massive medieval fortress.He decided to explore. In one of the cells he found a rust-pitted ring bolt set in the floor and there was a deep recess let into the stonework a few feet above. He put hand inside and pulled out some dusty cylinder-shaped things. Having stripped one of what seemed to be rotten skin he found rolls of grey cloth-like paper inside. There were traces of something written on the outer layer of the roll but what was there had long been unreadable. Where the underlying sheets began to be legible he found a script that hardly contrasted in colour with the material it was written on. After an extended examination back in Athens he found that the writing was Italian in the Venetian dialect of the Sixteenth Century. When he eventually pieced the fragments together, filling in gaps in the text as best he could, he produced the version translated below into English;

" " " " years ago - I cannot say how many - a Genovese merchant was brought to see me here in my cell. I could not profit from his visit. Unaccustomed to talking, I remained inarticulate in his presence. There was nothing about me that would have been useful in identifying me, even had he so wished. My Venetian dress disappeared long ago. Amputation of my left leg at some point early after my capture almost killed me, and left me less than human.

A spark of life must have remained in me - to be fanned into flame only to let me painfully spend long years of crawling on the stones of this cell, clawing at an axe that only exists in my fiercely impaired mind.

My forearms soon became as calloused as urchins' feet. I am a hairy freak that my special jailer once brought his friends to laugh at. There is not much human communication now, though plenty of contacts with rats: food is left most days and I fall upon it like an animal, moving the rats aside. Even that might be bearable, but I am always tortured by thirst. In the morning they set a small bowl of water just outside the radius that my hand can reach, with the chain cutting into my bleeding and festering ankle unmercifully. Towards evening they move it nearer but sometimes they forget. So when I sleep I dream of the spring by the remains of a temple near this fortress, described to me by a Greek priest who used come into my cell. He was a kindly man. My Turkish guards beheaded him for talking about the Holy Virgin of Perachora. Probably the temple was originally built over a holy spring dedicated to some goddess, perhaps Aphrodite of Greek antiquity. Such places elsewhere have become sanctuaries to the Madonna.

This dream always turns into a nightmare of fire as I have visions of hacking my way through flames, then wake to suffer another cruel day on these stones, roasting in summer or freezing in winter, but always waterless through the long day.

I remember the Genovese explaining that Italians were trading again with this part of the world, and that ships often came to nearby Corinth to discharge their cargoes to be horse-drawn across the isthmus. He said the Navy had had a great Victory a Navpactus-Lepanto - that was where we Venetians fought. He said that the Muslim invasion of Europe had been defeated for ever.

An idea came to me later - or was it the merchant who suggested it? It was that if I were to write everything down that I could remember I would be prepared to ask him more if he came back. I pleaded with the guards for writing materials. Months passed, and then one day some paper was thrown into my cell. It took further endless weeks before I could secure some pieces of graphite. The jailers laughed at me as I lay on the floor scrawling away month after month, destroying and re-writing where my mind had things out of time and place. They pointed their fingers at their temples and grinned at each other, but I grew more confident as no one tried to stop me writing.

Why do I struggle to write this in such pain? Is it to stop going mad with fretting over wrongs I have suffered? In saner moments I know that Francesco Valente, my father, will never see it, and will never know that it was not his son but some damned dolt enthralled by the Sanmichele family who secreted a girl in Admiral Veniero's

Flagship, risked the derision of the Venetian Fleet, and arrogantly brought upon himself the hatred of a Dominican friar and the ex-slave master Murad. He must know that I didn't desert the battle but fought well. I still hope to set my father's mind at rest on any question of the valour his son, and the minds of my Capodistrian boyhood friends. There were many accusations of cowardice in that great Fleet. The Spaniards in particular laid this charge against the Venetians long before the battle started. To escape battle many Spaniards too jumped into the sea where it was so shallow that some ships of the northern flank went aground. Knowing that I had disappeared from the Venetian Flagship did anyone deceive him, innocently or maliciously, saying that I had sought to keep my body whole by making for the shore? I struggle on here, a skeleton rattling on these cruel stones, so that some day he may know his son was never a coward.

I suppose the fire in the fire ship's basket didn't take a proper hold and the flames died out before I was burnt alive. My last recollection of this event is burns from my heated armour, which seemed little in comparison with the pain from my smashed leg, and a cruel striving for air. The fire ship would have drifted off through the thick fumes and onto the northern shore of the Gulf that was held by the Ottoman. Murad could hardly have followed the success or otherwise of his torched boat amongst all those floating flaming furnaces.

I am leaving these final lines with the rest of my work that lies in the dust behind the stone ledge above me. Neither that merchant, nor any other, ever came again. I expect to die here with what I have written. It is simply that there is no one any longer who has any responsibility for me. I am left to some jailers with whom I communicate only by signs, and they no longer trouble to close the door of my cell. The authorities? If authorities responsible for this fortress still exist they will be far away in Istanbul, and it seems that even my jailers have been forgotten or abandoned by them..."

Perhaps some peasants looting after the battle, finding me on the beach, took me for a Venetian nobleman from my armour, and sold me to the local Ottoman authority, or were forced to part with me because some official thought I might be worth ransom money. He and all others that have since handled my poor body were disappointed. My father, the only person with the means, and who would have had the inclination to ransom me, was most probably told.... what was he told??

Even if my love, Michaela, had been able later to inform Veniero, supposing they both survived the battle, Veniero would have found it difficult to believe and inform my father that a monk had murdered me, or tried to. My uncle, Marcantonio Sanmichele, has no doubt been politically ruined by Priuli, as well as being socially disgraced by his daughter's abandoned behaviour in running away to sea with me, and he can be in no position to help anyone.

I am leaving these final lines with the rest of my work that lies in the dust behind the stone ledge above me. Neither that merchant, nor any other, ever came again. I expect to die here with what I have written. It is simply that there is no one any longer who has any responsibility for me. I am left to some jailers with whom I communicate only by signs, and they no longer trouble to close the door of my cell. The authorities? If authorities responsible for this fortress still exist they will be far away in Istanbul, and it seems that even my jailers have been forgotten or abandoned by them..."

www.ingramcontent.com/pod-product-compliance
Ingram Content Group UK Ltd.
Pitfield, Milton Keynes, MK11 3LW, UK
UKHW041939190726
13854UKWH00004B/1673

9 781847 994714